The Girl With Strawberry Hair

The Liberty Saints, Volume 1

Michael Moore

Published by Michael Moore, 2023.

To Jennifer, who has always stood next to me, and to Jonathan and Ethan, who will make whatever corner of the Earth they live on a better place.

PREFACE

My first experience with westerns was probably around...1980. My family had just moved to Dallas, Texas, and my parents set up a black and white television in my bedroom, one of those gray and black thirteen-inch televisions with the knobs to change the channel. At the time outside of cartoons I wasn't allowed to watch anything else, and on Saturdays I would watch every cartoon possible until American Bandstand came on and you knew that was the end of fun entertainment for the day. One day, though, after Looney Tunes was over, my father came into my bedroom and changed the channel to one I hadn't gone to before. And there, on Channel 39, I saw the Lone Ranger for the first time. I was instantly engaged in the adventures of the masked man played by Clayton Moore and his faithful companion Tonto, played by the great Jay Silverheels. I loved the horses, the quick draw guns, the good guys bringing the bad ones to justice, and their ride-off at the end of each episode that guaranteed the adventures would continue. The adventures would continue for one more half-hour, and then after that came what would be my favorite, and the one that most influenced the book you have in front of you, *The Rifleman*. The Rifleman told the story of Lucas McCain and his young son Mark McCain, played by Chuck Conners and Johnny Crawford, respectively. Each week they would get into adventures, some funny, some suspenseful, many action-packed, but no matter what happened they both had each other. I gravitated to this one due to the relationship I had with my father, who has been and is still my best friend. I could fantasize about being Mark and my father being Lucas

McCain, since both men were larger than life, at least they were to me. Fast forward many years, and now I find myself in the Lucas McCain position, with a young son getting close to the age of Johnny Crawford when he first played young Mark. I thought about shows like *The Rifleman*, *Bonanza* (my second favorite) and *Have Gun Will Travel*, as well as John Wayne and Clint Eastwood westerns. So many great western stories, but I grew up never seeing someone with my skin color and hair on the small...and large screens, with the exception of some supporting roles here and there. I learned over time that African-Americans were not sitting on the sidelines of the Wild West, but were neck-deep in it, and were just as much a part of the tapestry of the Wild West as anyone. Men and women such as Bass Reeves, Stagecoach Mary, Bob Lemmons, Nat Love, Bill Pickett, Cathay Williams, Mary Ellen Pleasant, and many more helped make the reality of the Old West every bit as much as Wild Bill, Wyatt Earp, and Calamity Jane did, but it's only recently that the stories about the African-American heroes- and villains - have been told. I sat down to write this book as a fun fictional story for anyone to pick up and read, and hope that they will fall in love with the adventures of Jack Tarver and his son Chris as they find a new home and new adventures in the town of Liberty, where they make new friends and a few enemies along the way. I wrote this book for that little boy who sat on his rocking horse, and marveled at the black and white adventures of the heroes he saw on screen, dreaming that he, too, could someday wear a cowboy hat and ride across the west with his best friend, dispensing justice to the bad guys and carving his name into legend...

Chapter 1: Discovery at Virginia Hill

In which Jack Tarver loses a friend and finds himself surrounded by enemies he did not expect...

Sam Spivey gurgled what would soon be his last gasps, staring down at the three bullet holes that poked out from the now dirt-stained blue Union soldier uniform. He looked up, his brown eyes viewing the three soldiers looking down at him. He tried to smile, most of all at the young dark-skinned soldier looking down at him. He was tall man of a muscular but thin build, with a square jaw and hard brown eyes, and despite his youth already had a few wrinkles on his face. What was his name? Sam found himself wanting to laugh at the absurdity of suddenly not remembering his best friend's name...

"Sam! It's Jack, Sam! Can you hear me? Sam!" Jack said, looking down at his training buddy. Jack winced as he inspected the bullet wounds that ruined his friend. Sam was also just as tall as Jack, but thinner, and his thin black mustache quivered, as he understood that the end was truly near. Jack Tarver and Sam Spivey, the terrible two, their Sergeant had called them. Many of their fellow soldiers chided that they single handedly ended battles before everyone else had a chance to fight. Jack tried to smile as Sam silently responded to his voice, but he knew his friend was at his last moments. Jack and E Company had been scouting a nearby plantation named Virginia Hill, a few miles outside of Durham, North Carolina. It was a large white house with a small dirt road leading past the cotton field almost right to the door. It looked almost as if it had been recently repainted, and flowers of all colors were in full bloom around it, and a bell chime could be seen hanging from the porch nearby a swinging bench. Virginia Hill had belonged to Mathias and Shelly Virginia, who had lived at that house for twenty years before the war started, and they had quickly evacuated further south, taking their slaves with them as the fighting grew nearer. The war was effectively over, but there were still pockets of resistance, which brought E Company here, only a few months before they were due to return home to their respective families as they were part of the volunteer force. Sam had moved out in front of the rest of the group, as usual, always after the glory. He had just rounded out to the back of the home when a series of shots rang out, and the remaining company, most of whom went inside the house to get the assassins, rushed in, only to find that Sam's luck had just ran out. Two white soldiers, Jeremy Davis and Godfrey Miller, stood over Jack and Sam, and shook their heads. Jeremy was a large heavy set man with a large black beard, with dark eyes and a low brow, a man who almost always wore a scowl on his face, and adjusted his unkempt uniform as he peered down at Sam, and Godfrey was a lanky young black man with a long face and a brown handlebar mustache that just didn't look right to any one who saw it.

"That was a fool thing to do, Sam! You shoulda' waited!" said Jeremy, spitting some tobacco from the side of his mouth. How it never caught on his scruffy beard always escaped everyone. Jack never liked Jeremy, not just because of his habits, but his *other* habits: The kind that tortured captured soldiers before killing them. Godfrey, uncaring as always, shrugged his thin shoulders as he turned toward the house after several shots rang out. Seems they found the ambushers. Godfrey pulled out his gun and ran in through the white door as fast as his thin legs would carry him, while Jeremy tried to grab Jack by his shoulders, but Jack brushed him off.

"C'mon, Sam made a mistake that cost him. Won't do no good watching the fool die, Tarver!"

Jack shrugged off Jeremy and tried once again to get through to Sam-but found that he already had as Sam smiled and spoke through a waning voice.

"Had some fun, didn't we, Jack? Wish I could be there, you know, after your boy is born. I never been a godfather, I hoped that would buy me some currency with the Almighty, y'know? Ain't gonna happen now...Do me one thing, eh?"

"Whatever you want, Sam."

"I ain't got no real family, 'cept the townsfolk in Liberty, so tell them-and your boy- about me, okay? Don't let me be forgotten."

Jack brushed the tears from his eyes and nodded silently. Sam smiled, and looked into the cloudy sky.

"Looks like it's gonna rain. Took long enough."

Jack watched, noticing the confederate soldier sneaking up behind him, but he was determined to watch Sam pass to the next world. He saw the light finally leave Sam's eyes, and Jack closed Sam's eyelids. They started together, and now have ended together. Jack, with a reflex faster than lightning, grabbed Sam's pistol lying next to him, and spun around just in time to avoid the first bullet from the soldier. Jack fired off one shot, which was all that was needed as the soldier grabbed his chest in surprise and fell to the ground. Jack slowly stood up, took one last look at his best friend, and walked inside the house.

"Bad luck there, Jack! I actually liked Sam, but we got the one who killed him! ," one soldier said, running by Jack just as he entered the house, looking around as the other soldiers proceeded to ransack the house, grabbing anything that wasn't nailed down. Jack looked toward the window facing the back of the house, and saw a Confederate soldier lying crumpled by the window that faced out right where Sam had fallen. Jack shook his head in acceptance, and inquired as to where Jeremy and Godfrey were at, and eventually made his way upstairs to the master bedroom, where he happened in on the pair as they were looking at what looked like a map. Jack nearly tripped over the dead body of another Confederate soldier at his feet, and glanced at the map. Jeremy tried to move the map away, but was too late as Jack saw a part of it. Jeremy thought better of it and opened the entire map to Jack after exchanging a glance with Godfrey.

"So what's this? That's Colorado territory...this looks like some sort of treasure map!"

"So what makes you think that?"

"I've read some reports about Confederate gold being lost, some to us, to the Injuns, some to just bad luck, and others that got hid..."

Godfrey pretended to look, shaking his head.

"So there's gold there. Wonder how much?"

Jeremy smiled.

"Enough to make us kings, Godfrey! With this gold-"

Jack stood up, his six-foot four-inch height looming over both men.

"We have to give that to Captain Davies! *If* there is gold there, that money can help us rebuild-"

Jeremy shook his head, because he knew this would happen, from the despicable heart-of-gold Jack Tarver, no less.

"Rebuild *what*? The South can do that on their own, they cost us enough. And we freed ya'll, so we don't owe you nuthin'! But this gold can set the three of us straight for a long time! No reason we should come out of this war empty-handed! We ain't gonna be war heroes, but at least we'll be rich!"

Jack shook his head and tightened his grip on his gun, slowly raising it up.

"What the hell do you plan to do, Negro? You gonna shoot me for it? Learn him, Godfrey!"

Jack hadn't noticed how Godfrey had silently gotten behind him, and hit Jack over the back of his head with the butt of his gun, and Jack fell forward, hitting the nightstand as he fell, knocking over a lamp filled with oil. The lamp crashed on the wooden floor the same time Jack hit the ground, clumsily firing a shot as he hit the floor. Jeremy jumped as the shot ricocheted off of the bedpan near his foot, and Jeremy began to draw his gun before noticing that the spark from the bedpan had ignited the oil, and the fire spread quickly over to the flower pattern window curtain, and moved up the curtain like a python. Godfrey ran toward the door, before calling back to Jeremy.

"Hell! Let's go, Jeremy!"

Jeremy didn't need the prompting as he made his way to the door. Just as he tried to step over Jack, he discovered that Jack wasn't quite finished yet, reaching up and tripping Jeremy, who fell to the floor like a sack of potatoes. Godfrey cursed through the smoke that now inundated the room, and ran down the stairs, telling the men that a confederate was hiding upstairs and started a fire. Jeremy and Jack struggled on the floor, first with each other, and then for control of the map. The smoke and flames made it difficult to see, and Jeremy hit Jack repeatedly with the butt of his gun to break his hold on him, but not before Jack grabbed the map and tore it from Jeremy's hands. Jeremy cursed this as he hit Jack one more time, finally knocking him out, and got up but couldn't see for the smoke, which now stung his eyes to the point of barely being able to see. Jeremy took one step closer, and then decided it wasn't worth it, and headed downstairs. At least Tarver would die with the map...

Jack coughed as he felt the heat from the flames all around him. He could just barely hear the galloping horses as the company rode away. He shook his head, and felt the warm blood and sweat that coursed down the side of his head. Jack stood up, unable to see, much less gauge where the door was located. The flames surrounded the entire room, and Jack could feel the floor beginning to buckle from the flames. He quickly stashed the map in his coat pocket and stomped on the floor. It was either brilliance or the last move of a desperate man, but Jack was determined to live, if for nothing more than to get home to Elizabeth.

Jack kept stomping, even as he felt the fire begin to lick at his boots. A loud snapping sound confirmed what Jack was hoping for, and one last stomp sent Jack barreling down with a section of the floor to find himself landing in the living room. Jack quickly got up and ran out of the now burning house and stumbled to the ground as he reaches Sam's body. He felt the cold sprinkles of the rain's opening salvo hit his face. He almost laughed at the timing of it, but for the realization that he almost died-at the hands of his own men, even if they were White. Jack looked over at Sam, almost wanting to ask Sam to sing one of those songs he was so fond of. Jack shook his head and stood up. He would reckon with Jeremy and Godfrey later. First he had to take care of his friend. Jack carefully wrapped Sam's body in his sleeping bag, and tied Sam's body onto the saddle of his horse, and made the lonely journey back to Fort Wayne, and along the way made a decision about the map he now had in his possession...

May 10th, 1865

It was recorded in the Fort Wayne books that Corporal Jack Tarver returned from seeming death at the Virginia Falls Plantation with news of the Betrayal of Jeremy Davis and Godfrey Miller after the ambush that killed Corporal Sam Spivey. The Military Court under General John Parke found Davis and Miller guilty of conspiring to murder Jack Tarver, and were sentenced to 10 years of hard labor in Desert Falls Prison, Nevada. Jack Tarver requested early resignation from the United States Military, which was granted by Captain William Smith for outstanding service to his country. Jack Tarver left Fort Wayne, taking with him what many say was Sam Spivey's most prized possession, a modified Smith and Wesson pistol of a slightly strange design.

The armed forces wish Jack Tarver long life and health.

Lieutenant Patrick Jackson

Fort Wayne, Virginia

Chapter 2: Liberty

In which Jack Tarver arrives at Sam Spivey's hometown 10 years later, with a heavy heart and boy in tow.

"Are we there yet?"

Jack shook his head in the negative for the fifth time that day as the rickety wagon full of home furnishings lurched forward down what seemed like the same stretch of dirt road and farmlands for the last several days. He looked from under his beige hat, his eyes, now with creases that didn't used to be there, looked at his son and managed a small grin. Chris was eleven years old now, his skin a very light brown, with black hair like his mothers', and her soft brown eyes too. Chris was a strong boy for his age, from Jack having him help with the chores as soon as he was able. Jack also saw the sad face, which must have come from him. He and Elizabeth did the best they could with Chris, even after Doc Samson diagnosed Elizabeth with a heart condition Jack couldn't even pronounce, much less understand. He and Chris had ten good years with Elizabeth before she died. Jack looked back to the road ahead. After she passed, there was no way they could live in that house, and Jack remembered Sam Spivey's hometown of Liberty, and all the wonderful things he said about it. Apparently they welcomed Negroes there. Jack had kept his word and told Chris all about his godfather Sam, and sent a letter back to Liberty about Sam not long after he died. Jack decided he would look up a few of Sam's friends. Sam would have wanted that. Chris nearly jumped out of his seat as he pointed toward the sign ahead.

"Look Pa! We've arrived in Liberty!"

Sure enough, the sign welcomed them to Liberty. Jack noted how nice the sign looked. Must have a good artisan, which Jack took as an encouraging sign of the town's virility. Jack looked around at the various farmlands and graze country they passed by. He especially noted a small, empty looking ranch just east of the road.

"Now when we get to town Chris, I want you to stay close until I can get a room at the hotel, and even after that, you stay close until I say otherwise. We're strangers here, and so are they. I know you're not prone to trouble, but it does tend to find young boys!"

"Aw, I won't get into any trouble!"

"I know, 'cause you'll be right beside me!"

Jack pointed to the ranch he had been staring at.

"What do you think about that place?"

Chris looked and shrugged his shoulders.

"Looks okay, Pa, but why ask me?"

"Well, we're a family, and it should be a family decision as to where we live. If your mother were here she'd have her say as well-"

"You mean we would live where she wanted to."

"Exactly."

Jack chuckled a bit at this, and Chris was glad to see something resembling a smile cross his father's face. Since his mother died, Chris hasn't seen his father do too much smiling. Chris loved his mother, and knew how much his Father loved her, the way he looked at her, and the retreat into himself after she died. He was always there for Chris, but even Chris could feel his father grow distant, especially with their neighbors. He stopped talking to them, almost distrusting them. Not that he ever really did to begin with. Chris remembered that his mother had told him that Jack experienced something toward the end of the war that caused that distrust, but never said more than that. Chris took out his slingshot and shot a few leaves off of trees as they passed by. He dared not shoot at an animal, as that would surely draw the ire of his father, who looked at it like torture.

A few men soon passed by on wagons and horseback, and all nodded and tipped their hats as they passed by.

Jack looked ahead a few minutes later and saw the town just ahead. Still growing, but not too fast. He could already make out the general store and the barbershop. There seemed to be a good amount of folk on the street, not surprising on a beautiful day like today. The wagon soon arrived in town, passing the various shops and stores; all seem to be doing well. Men and women lined the streets, going about their daily businesses. The people looked curiously at Chris and Jack, but not unfriendly. A few children ran alongside the wagon and asked about Chris, and Jack allowed Chris to speak with them. The boy should start making friends fast. That should take away some of the stress of starting over. Jack soon stopped the wagon just outside of a building that had this sign:

BILLY BURROUGHS: LAND APPRAISAL FOR LIBERTY

Jack stepped off of the wagon first, and Chris leaped off the other side of the wagon recklessly and fell to his knees in a cloud of dust. Jack shook his head disapprovingly, but said nothing as he entered the office. Chris got up and ran after him, bumping into a kind older man as he ran.

"I'm sorry, sir!"

Marshal Elijah Bronson noticed the two new strangers the moment they entered town. The boy didn't concern Elijah so much as the man carrying a familiar looking gun in his holster. Liberty hasn't had any trouble in the twenty-two years that Elijah had been marshal. Which suited his wife Stella just fine. Elijah was just passing the age of fifty-five, and was a man of average height, but a commanding man, and still had a decent gun hand, but found it unnecessary to use it. He used his wrinkled hands for more practical things, like stopping spirited young boys in their tracks.

"Not a problem. What's your name, son?"

"Chris Tarver."

"Well met, son. I'm Elijah Bronson, town marshal. You and your pa moving here?"

"Yessir!"

Jack walked out of the office the moment he realized that Chris didn't follow him in. He looked over at Chris disapprovingly.

"Chris, I thought I told you to stay close."

Elijah raised his hands in guilt.

"Sorry, Mr. Tarver, I held Chris up. I just wanted to welcome our newest residents. I'm Elijah Bronson."

Jack shook hands with Elijah and Elijah glanced at the gun handle in Jack's holster. Elijah almost let out a hoot.

"Mr. Tarver-"

"Jack."

"Jack, I recognize that gun! Smith and Wesson, with a modified hammer and trigger. Only one man I knew ever had one like it. Sam Spivey!"

"Yeah, I served with Sam toward the end of the war. I was there when he passed."

Elijah smiled. So this was Jack Tarver.

"Sam mailed letters back regularly to us, and told all about a young black man named Jack he became friends with. Sam lost his mother and father to fire when he was small, but the whole town took care of him. We were so proud when he left to fight..."

Jack smiled. He liked Elijah already. Chris stood eyes transfixed on Elijah's silver badge.

"Yeah, that gun was modified by the smithy, Miles Jepson. He'll be glad to see that gun again. Work of art, he always called it."

Jack motioned for Chris to enter the land office, and tipped his hat to Elijah.

"Well, maybe I'll pay him a visit later. Thank you, Marshal Bronson. Good day."

"To you as well, Jack. Don't worry; Billy will give you a fair deal. This is a great place to live. Fine place to raise your boy."

With that Jack left Elijah to his daily walk and went in to find their new home. It didn't take long.

Doctor Howard Harrison tipped his hat and twirled his silver mustache and he passed a pretty young woman with golden hair and wearing a new pink dress. Doc Harrison always loved the ladies, and they him, until old age moved him along. The doctor soon found himself arriving at his office at the same time as Sheriff Bronson.

"What's the good word, Elijah?"

Elijah smiled, the kind of smiled that always seemed to accompany important news.

"This and that, Doc, this and that. How's the Granger boy?"

"Oh, he'll be fine. The broken leg will heal quickly, as it does for all boys. He'll think twice before trying to break his father's prized horse, I'll tell you that!"

Doc Harrison entered his tidy office and placed his hat on it's worn wooden hook, and walked to his desk and sat down, Elijah sat down at the seat across from him and regarded him for a moment, not saying a word. Doc knew what that meant.

"I take it you aren't here about the Granger boy?"

Elijah shrugged his shoulders, and took off his hat, and ran a hand through his short gray hair.

"Just some information you might find interesting. A man named Jack Tarver just arrived here, looking to buy some land. It seems he was with Sam, you know, when he died in the War. I'm not entirely sure, but I think he's the same man who sent the letter about Sam. "

Doc Harrison stopped dead in his tracks, old memories washing over him like a tidal wave. It always seemed like yesterday to him and his wife Mary. Since Sam left...

"Thank you for the information, Elijah. Maybe I'll pay Mr. Tarver a visit after he gets settled in."

Elijah nodded his agreement. Besides, any man would want to know what happened to his only son, adopted or no...

"C'mon, Jim! I gotta have that money! You know what this means to me and Patricia!"

Jim Daley looked up at Clancy Miller from behind his desk and tried to think of what he could say. Jim was a soft-spoken man now entering his fortieth year with blonde hair that was betraying tufts of gray throughout as Father Time truly began his march, which was also starting to invade his perfectly cut goatee. Thankfully he kept himself in shape even with a slight build. His soft blue eyes took a quick look through the glass of the door that separated his office from the other patrons of Liberty Bank. He then glanced down at the various handmade toys his three children had made for him, to "decorate" his drab oak desk. Jim straightened his newly tailored black suit he just received from New York and looked at Clancy sadly, and wondered what had become of the man he knew. Jim had known Clancy and Patricia ever since they came to Liberty as that bright-eyed couple ten years ago. That was before their eleven-year-old daughter Helen contracted pneumonia several weeks ago. Her condition had worsened, and not even Doc Harrison could do anything for her. Some fancy medicine in New York could help her, but it was expensive. Jim appraised the Miller home, but would only cover half the cost of the medicine and the cost to deliver it to Liberty. Clancy looked pleadingly through sunken blue eyes, scratching his short dirty blonde hair, ever hopeful. He looked ragged and his clothes were dusty from doing small ranch work here and there, where he could find it. Jim shook his head again.

"I'm sorry Clancy. I can't help you. I wish I could, I truly do. Land prices aren't what they used to be, you know. Ranching's where it's at right now. I'll see what I can do, but for right now I can't help you."

Clancy gripped his hat until it looked like it would explode. Clancy looked up through tearful eyes, with the look of betrayal on his face.

"Dammit, Jim, you know my little girl. You know Helen! Refusin' us like this. It's like you killed her yerself! Don't know how you can sleep at night, you vulture!"

Clancy looked around, as if trying do something, and looked at Jim one last time and then stormed out of the room.

"I'll fix you, Jim! You'll pay for this!"

Jim tried to go back to work, but set his papers down and looked at the spot where Clancy stood. Jim then left for the telegraph office. Maybe there was something he could do after all.

"This is great! Look at this, Pa!"

Chris had already leaped off the wagon and ran around to the back of what was formerly the Crowley House. It was a small gray house, with three rooms, which was all Jack and Chris needed. The Crowleys had kept the house well maintained before moving to California. Fifteen acres of land surrounded the house, and Jack had already looked at the fence, and saw where there would need to be some repair before cattle could graze, but that wasn't unexpected. Jack was surprised the home and land was as good a condition as it was, and to be sold to a Negro, there was good reason to be skeptical. There was Grant Henderson's field next to theirs, but he heard that Henderson was a good and fair man, which was a good sign for them. Jack walked into the home and was almost surprised to find that the Smiths left the dinner table and chairs there. No luck with the bed, but Jack had those in the back of the wagon. Jack used his brown hat to wipe some of the standing dust from the wooden chair and sat at the table, glad for a moment of stillness. Elizabeth always respected these moments for him, which was just another reason he loved her so much. This would make a great home, but there was one last person to ask. Fortunately, Chris ran into the home in a case of perfect timing.

"Pa, Pa, this place is great! There's a creek just a bit ways back, and there's a tree house, and..."

"Slow down, Chris! You'll die of joy! So I take it this is the place for us?"

Chris smiled.

So did Jack.

They were home!

Chapter 3: The King of Aces

In which life around Liberty starts to get interesting when the gambler comes to town, and draws the ire of the local cattle baron...

"We're comin' up on Liberty, folks!" said the stage driver, looking to the town ahead. Alan Gentry, known around many parts as Blackjack, straightened his gray tie, and tipped his hat at the pretty lady sitting across from him. He had spoken to her as soon as she had entered the stage not two days ago. Her name was...Miss...ah! Miss Ellie Stanton. She was a beautiful statuesque red-haired woman, just coming back from a school in San Francisco. Young, not much older than twenty-two, Gentry figured. She cocked one of her eyebrows in amusement as she smiled at him. She leaned forward and put a hand on his leg.

"My dear Mr. Gentry—"

"Call me Blackjack, ma'am."

"Blackjack. We're almost in town. Where will you stay?"

"I live my life out of hotels, Ms. Stanton. Perhaps you'd like to dine with me tonight?"

Ellie pulled back and seemed to think it over for a moment, and then laughed out loud.

"Ah, my, you never know when to quit, do you? However do you make you're living playing cards?"

Blackjack smiled at Ellie. She would be tougher than he thought. But would it be interesting any other way?

"Carefully, ma'am, carefully. Sometimes it's at that moment of quitting when victory can be taken," he said, and looked out of the window as shops and businesses started to appear outside of the carriage window. He took note of the hotel and the saloon, and the people walking around. Ranching and cattle raising was getting popular around here, and money was everywhere, if you knew who to take it from...

Elijah took his hat off and wiped the dust from it as he walked from the barbershop toward the stage. He saw Archer Stanton standing by the stage stop, with two of his ranch hands. Elijah figured that Ellie Stanton had finally returned to Liberty, since Mr. Stanton rarely seemed to leave his ranch. Elijah walked across the street as the stagecoach came to a stop, not far away from him. Elijah shook hands with Timmy the stagehand, and walked around the stage just as Ellie ran into her father's arms. It had been a four years since she went to that girls' school, and certainly they took the tomboy right out of her. Elijah shook his head and smiled. He remembered when she was just tall enough to look at his belt buckle. Ellie hugged Archer and kissed him on the cheek, and then hugged the ranch hands, Pedro and Esteban, who had worked for her father since her mother died so long ago. Elijah was about to welcome Ellie back when he noticed the other passenger stepping off of the stage. A man of dark features, wearing a gray suit and hat, both looked to be brand new. He had steely blue eyes and black hair. He was clean-shaven, and his handsome face glanced at Elijah and he tipped his hat. Elijah shook his head in disgust. He had to be a gambler. Just what this town *doesn't* need. Elijah straightened his posture and stepped in from of the man, who went ahead and introduced himself.

"Well, you must be the town sheriff. I am Alan Gentry, known around parts as Blackjack."

"Must be nice being named after an object used to beat people. I'm Elijah Bronson, also known as Marshal Bronson. So how long are you staying? Better yet, when are you leaving?"

Blackjack smiled. This was going to be fun.

"Oh, however long the money lasts, Marshal, and from the looks of the kindly townsfolk here, that could be a while. Could you be a good man and show me where the barbershop is? I could use a trim."

Elijah pointed toward the barbershop and Gentry looked over and grabbed the fancy leather bag that was left next to him and started walking in that direction when Elijah put a hand on his shoulder. Blackjack took note that while he was old, the Marshal was still tough. He couldn't move forward, so he decided to play it off. Might as well hear the speech now.

He turned his head toward Elijah to show he had his attention.

"I know you're a gambler. I've heard of you. I hear you run a clean game, and that's good, because these are good people who work hard for that money. I also know you've been involved in a few gunfights over cards. Particularly the incident in Carson City." Elijah said, looking at Blackjack hard as he said this. He could feel Blackjack bristle at the mention of Carson City. Elijah took his hand off of his shoulder.

"What happened there won't be tolerated here. So help me, if you mess up once I'll run you right out of town on a crippled donkey. Now get about your business."

Blackjack started walking toward the Barbershop, and turned to give Elijah a bow, and continued on. This was going to be fun indeed.

The evening came by quickly at the Old Yellow saloon, and Elijah found himself walking in. It was the first night of Blackjack in Liberty, and so far it was a peaceful one. Elijah came in to make sure it stayed that way. The saloon was busier than normal, maybe because of Blackjack's reputation. It certainly wasn't hurting Harvey the bartender too much. Elijah took a post at the far end of the bar, and Harvey came by as quickly as he could and offered Elijah a drink. Elijah raised his hand to refuse, and Harvey flashed a quick smile and went back to serving what was turning into quite a crowd of people. Elijah peered over at the table where Blackjack sat, involved in a game with, among other people, Clancy Miller. Elijah shook his head. He had heard about Clancy's blow up at the bank the day before. He had hoped that something could be done, and he thought for sure the banker was doing something to help, but Clancy at a poker game? The situation must be worse than he thought. Clancy wiped the sweat from his brow. He had already lost fifty dollars. He needed a win badly, and he knew it. Everyone else had folded, and it was just Clancy and Blackjack. Blackjack looked up, legs crossed and flashed that smile that made women swoon, and men want to shoot him. Clancy had a two pair. Surely the game was his! He threw two more ten dollars in. That made the bet sixty dollars.

"All right, Blackjack, show me your hand!"

"By all means, Mr. Miller, you first."

Clancy smiled. He had him!

Blackjack looked down at the table as Clancy threw down his two pair. Blackjack smiled and shrugged his shoulders. Clancy stood up and triumphantly started to pull the mountain of coins and cash toward him when Blackjack grabbed his arm, and showed him his cards.

It was a full house.

Clancy looked at the cards in disbelief. He simply stared at them as Blackjack moved the money toward him. Clancy shook his head. More money lost that was needed for Helen. Clancy looked up at the smiling Blackjack. He whispered the words first. Elijah raised himself and started to make his way to the table. He didn't hear what Clancy had said, but he didn't have to. For that matter no one did, especially Blackjack, whose hand moved to the handle of his pearl-handled gun. Clancy's hand also went to his gun.

"Cheat."

"Now hang on, I run a clean game, Mr. Miller. If you couldn't afford it, you shouldn't have come here."

Clancy uttered Helen's name as he began to draw his pistol, not hearing the footsteps of Elijah behind him. Blackjack drew his gun faster than lightening and actually pointed it at Clancy before his gun had cleared the holster. Elijah grabbed Clancy and lifted him up, taking his gun away in the process.

"That's enough, Clancy. There was no cheating here. Go home!"

Blackjack motioned to Clancy with his gun.

"Listen to the Marshal there, my friend. I guarantee you'll live longer."

Clancy struggled a moment more as the patrons watched in amusement. One of the other men sitting at that table, a tall Mexican with a long mustache and sunken features seemed to agree with Clancy, and quickly raised his gun to take advantage of the fact that Blackjack had been watching Clancy. Blackjack had thought if anyone would, it would have been him. Blackjack swirled in his chair and shot at the man first, and the bullet struck him squarely in the chest. The man clutched his chest, wheezed for a moment, and then landed dead on the table, scattering coins and dollars everywhere. The entire saloon went dead, and everyone simply stared. Even Clancy and Elijah stopped struggling with each other. Everyone looked first to the dead man, and then up to Blackjack, who nonchalantly lit a cigar. Elijah let go of Clancy, who looked at the dead man and ran out of the saloon. Elijah was at least glad for that, and turned to address the patrons, all of whom looked stunned.

"The show's over, people! Go back to your drinking or go home!" Elijah said, and turned his attention to the dead man on the floor. Blackjack moved his winnings into his bag and stood up. It appears he was done for the night. He took one more glance at Elijah and the dead man.

"Not that I care terribly, Marshal, but do you know that man?"

"Yes I do. Esteban Morales. He's one of the ranch hands at the Stanton spread."

"Really? Well, give Miss Ellie my condolences. It was a fair killing, and you know it."

Elijah stood up as Harvey and another man helped lift the dead man and carry him to the caretakers'.

"I'll agree to that, but we'll let Judge Harper make that decision. I'd be more concerned about what Archer Stanton thinks. That was one of his best men."

"Well, thanks for the warning, Marshal. I'll be at the hotel if you need me."

"Fine, as long as you don't try to leave town."

"Perish the thought."

With that Blackjack left the saloon, nodding at a few people as he passed. Elijah looked on as the dead man was carried away. This was excitement this town just doesn't need. At least that new rancher and his boy probably won't cause any trouble...

Blackjack sat in his hotel room for what seemed like hours sipping some bourbon he had brought from Carson City by way of San Francisco. He sat in a chair facing the door, gun and bottle by the small table next to him. He was used to nights like this, as vigilance and non-sleep were also the hallmarks of the gambling life. He debated how much longer he wanted to stay awake. He had seen and dealt with men like Stanton before. No matter the reason Stanton would take the killing of his man personally, and would no doubt sent a party to take care of him. Tonight, or worse, at an undetermined time. Blackjack cursed that man for drawing his gun. He hadn't been in town a day and already found himself in trouble. But then again, was that really any different from anywhere else, he mused to himself. He was so deep in his own thoughts he almost missed the whispers coming from down below his window. Blackjack perked his ears, and then walked quietly over to the open window to listen in.

"He's right up there! Let's go kill him!" the first voice said.

"No way. We got a job to do soon! Get revenge on your own time. Not as if you're good enough to kill him anyway!" said the second voice.

"Don't matter. Between him and that no good banker..."

"Look, we take the money we get 'em all back! Get a grip, Clancy! Go back home to Patricia and Helen!"

The voices faded down the alley as Blackjack continued to listen. After he could hear no more he sat back down and continued his vigilance of the door. It was at least good to know the local drunk wouldn't try to kill him tonight...

Archer Stanton slowly walked to his study, just after the Marshal had been by to deliver the bad news. Esteban was dead, killed by the new gambler in town. Archer had no doubt that the Marshal was telling the truth that Esteban tried to shoot first, but it didn't matter. It was the principle of the matter, after all.

Archer began writing a note for Esteban's family in Mexico. He would have to tell Ellie what happened, and he had no doubt she would not take it very well. Esteban had been a friend to Ellie since she was little, teaching her how to ride a horse and even shoot a gun. Ellie would be greatly saddened, and a sad Ellie was more than enough for Archer to kill a man over. But the time wasn't right. Not yet.

Chapter 4: Shadows in the Sun

In which Jack and Chris begin anew in Liberty, little knowing the shadows that dance ever closer...

"Ma'am, can I see Helen?"

Patricia Miller was happy to see that some people weren't afraid to see Helen. What she didn't suspect was that it would come from someone who only started living in Liberty a few weeks ago. She smiled down at young Chris Tarver and motioned for him to come in. He had come by at least once week for the last several weeks, since he found out from the Peacock brothers that Helen was ill. A good boy from a good home. She would have to bake a pie for Chris and his father. She couldn't imagine a home without a mother, and knew those two could use a woman's touch. She noticed that Chris held what looked like a freshly carved wooden horse.

"Is that for Helen, Chris?"

"Why yes it is, ma'am. How is she?"

"She's the same. I'm not sure what else to do but pray to the Lord. Clancy, bless his soul, goes out for work every day to try to afford that medicine, but we're running out of time for her. I hoped her fever would break soon..."

Chris smiled, as he always did, and made his way toward Helen's room. Clancy came in a few seconds later, looking tired as always. What Patricia noticed today was the defiant glint Clancy had in his eyes, and for some reason she didn't like it one bit. Clancy took his hat off and sat down, looking at Helen's door as it closed.

"That the Tarver boy again, Patty?"

Patricia nodded her head, and saw Clancy smile toward the door, a good and honest smile she hasn't seen since Helen became sick.

"He's a good boy, that Tarver. His Pa raised him right. Can't say the same for the other little fools in this town. None of them will even come near Helen, or us for that matter."

Patty sat down in her favorite rocking chair, the one Clancy made right before they got married, and began knitting in silence. Every day since that day Clancy went to the bank, he's spoken more venom toward Liberty and its people. She understood why, but had hoped he might deal with the anger, but that hasn't happened. Whatever it was, Clancy was drifting farther and farther away from her and Helen. She had a bad feeling about Clancy, one that grew worse every day.

"Thanks for coming, Chris, and thanks for the horse. It's so detailed..."

Chris took off his hat as he sat in the familiar stool next to Helen's bed. Chris was never comfortable here, since this was, after all, a girl's room. The various dolls on her bed and dresser seemed to stare right at him. Helen looked from the horse to Chris and back again, a smile moving over her freckled face. Her cheeks were sunken, her hazel eyes red and tired-looking, but nevertheless had energy behind them that no sickness could stifle. Her mother had kept her bright red hair tied in a ponytail. She could feel that Chris was uncomfortable, but was glad he came, as always. She wished she could leave, and play with him and the others by the creek behind the Tarver home. She took a deep breath, not wanting to say what she knew she had to.

"You know I love it when you come to visit, Chris. No one else comes here, 'cause they're afraid of getting sick. I'm not getting any better, and I'm afraid now of you getting sick as well. I don't think you should come back."

Chris looked up as if he had been shot.

"But Helen, If I leave-"

"If you leave, then you won't get sick. I don't want to think of you getting sick, Chris. We're friends, and we always will be, whether I'm here or not. This is hard for me too. It's usually Ma and me here. Pa is always working, or trying to find it. Just stay with me for this last time, okay? After that, hopefully I'll see you again. Now if I remember, I'm up two games of tic tac toe..."

Helen smiled at Chris once more, and he marveled at her strength, and hoped that he would see her soon indeed...

It was a beautiful night sky that Bryce Daniels was happy about the most on a day that was anything but. Daniels rode down the dirt road with Barry Swenson and Paul Stevens, headed for the meeting that had been brewing for the last several weeks. Daniels had just lost his land to the bank, as they all had, and it was time for action. It was his land. His, and he was being cheated from it, and by all that's holy he swore he would kill to get it back, and he knows that promise is about to come true. His tired brown eyes looked up the road at the rider, who had a few other men with him coming near them. His dark features bristled as a cool wind blew through his thin shirt. Soon the riders were upon them, and Daniels decided to break the silence.

"So here we are. Don't expect to be bothered this time o' night. The plan is set. We got everything we need?"

"Humph. As if we need anything else. Everyone armed and carryin'?"

Swenson and Stevens looked at each other and then nodded in unison. Daniels did the same.

"Of course. I take it you are too?"

"Yeah. Tomorrow we gonna get ours. For our families!"

Clancy Miller smiled. He would get that money for his daughter's medicine. Damn that banker, and anyone else who stands in his way. Evil as it was, it was for Helen. His trip to Hell would be worth it.

It had been a grueling past few days for Jeremy Davis. He had been released from prison a few months ago and soon reunited with Godfrey in a small town near Fort Smith, Arkansas. He and Godfrey tried to make a go of it, working honest jobs, but before long they, along with a few others, turned to crime. A few banks here and there, and they were always able to lose them in the Oklahoma territory, which was Indian country no small town sheriff or federal marshal wanted any part of. Jeremy snorted as he and his group of seven men just left the home of Dennis Mayweather. The significance of this was that it was the former home, up until a month ago, of Jack and Elizabeth Tarver. It seemed that no one knew where he or his boy went to, either. Jeremy knew that Tarver had that map, and no doubt already taken the confederate gold there, and for all they knew had spent it all. Not that it mattered, because Jeremy was determined to get his money from Tarver, and either way, Tarver would be dead. It was just a matter of finding him. Godfrey looked back at the home they were leaving, and then looked to Jeremy.

"So what now, Jeremy? Where do we look?"

"How the hell am I supposed to know, butt knocker? We'll do what we been doin', robbin' banks and such. You heard of Tarver's rep. He's too good a man to lay low for long. Somewhere, sometime he'll help someone, and we'll all know it. Just have faith in the goodness of the man. I do."

The other men grumbled as Jeremy said this, but Jeremy was a patient man. He would wait for as long as he had to.

He didn't have to wait long...

Chris tried on the new red shirt Pa had gotten for him a few weeks ago. School was set to start within the next week, something Chris wasn't at all looking forward to. He had gotten to know a few of the boys his age in town, and of course Helen Miller. The Peacock brothers had said that schoolmarm Nancy Carroll was mean-she even punished a kid by making him drink castor oil for misspelling a word. Chris shivered at this thought.

"Chris! Let's go! How much longer do you need to get ready?" Jack called from outside. Chris tucked in his shirt and ran outside, to find Jack waiting for him in the wagon, looking somewhat displeased.

"We have a long day ahead of us, Chris! I have to go to the general store for feed, I have to enroll you in school, open a bank account...Maybe I should wake you earlier, if you need to take so much time to get ready?"

"Sorry, Pa."

"I'm not angry, Chris, I'm just glad you *can* go to school. I imagine if I had been able to go to school I wouldn't look forward to meeting the schoolteacher, either. Besides, the sooner we get done, the sooner we head to that fishing hole you found last week."

Chris brightened at this notion. This might be a good day after all.

Jim Daley had just put on another new gray suit, just arrived from San Francisco, and walked down the busy street of Liberty, nodding his gray hat, also from San Francisco, at the ladies as he walked by. He arrived at the Post Office and checked with Howard Burroughs. He was told the stage was scheduled to arrive today, and the new mail with it, but wasn't there yet. Jim thanked Howard and walked into the general store, where he saw the new family in town, Jack Tarver and his son, who was eyeing a jar full of licorice. Jim smiled and walked up to Jack.

"Hello, Mr. Tarver! I'm sorry I haven't had a chance to speak with you when you first arrived! I'm Jim Daley, bank manager for Liberty! This must be your son?"

Jack eyed Daley critically, but shook the outstretched hand.

"Yes, this is Chris. You'll have to forgive him; he's become transfixed by that jar of candy there. Chris!"

Chris was shaken from his reverie and shook Jim's hand.

"Pleased to meet you, sir!"

"Pleasure's mine, son. You and your father should come by and open an account."

Jack smiled, nodding his head.

"Well, Mr. Daley, we do have plans to head over there after I finish up here."

"Excellent! Well, how about this, why don't we open an account for both of you? You're never too young to start saving money, Chris!"

Jack looked at Chris and nodded his head in agreement.

"He's got a point, Chris. Why not take that licorice money and open an account?"

Jim smiled as he looked at Chris, who looked from him to the candy jar and back again.

Tough decisions for eleven-year-old boys.

"Chris, just for opening an account you get a free licorice from my jar!"

Chris brightened up at this, and Jack smiled at Chris.

"So you get the best of both worlds, Chris! Mr. Daley, are you heading to the bank soon?"

"Why, I'm going right now! Chris, would you like to come and open that account with me?"

Chris looked to Jack, who nodded his head. Jim laughed and tipped his hat to Jack.

"We'll be right back, Mr. Tarver! Maybe I can interest your son in the banking business!"

"You go right ahead, Mr. Daley! I have to go see Miles about some modifications to my gun, but I'll be there soon. You two have fun!"

Jack watched as Chris and Jim left the general store to make their way toward the bank. Jim was so busy telling Chris all about the advantages of having his own account he didn't notice that they were both being watched by an anxious Clancy Miller, who stroked his gun. It couldn't be more perfect. Sheriff Bronson had been called away to the Hart farm for a theft report, and wouldn't be back for a few hours.

Clancy walked around to the side of the Old Yellow Saloon and met with Daniels, who watched the bank from an alley by the building. Daniels nodded to the six others in the shadows behind him.

"There's that bank dandy! Let's get this over with. Stick to the plan, and we'll be rich!"

Daniels looked away from Miller, and nodded to the others. No point in splitting the money seven ways, when six takes you further...

Chris soon found himself chomping vigorously on the black licorice stick as he barely heard Mr. Daley, between chewing, as he explained the intricacies of the banking business. As long as they included candy, Chris was all for it. Mr. Daley finished writing the first account for Chris Tarver, and then asked Chris to sign the account, and Chris was pleased to hand over his money for savings, and he figured that since he got to keep the money and get the licorice, he's had a good day. He started hearing the sounds of some sort of commotion going on outside of the office, and Mr. Daley motioned for Chris to stay seated while he found out what was happening. Chris sat for a few moments, and jumped out of his chair as he heard a gunshot. Chris stood for a moment, frozen in place, unsure as to what to do next. He walked slowly toward the door, and cracked it open. He saw the kind Mr. Daley sprawled on the floor, clutching his shoulder with an old woman kneeling next to him, and other bank patrons with their hands up, and seven men wearing bandanas over their faces pointing guns at them. Chris gripped his licorice tighter, as one of the masked men, wearing a brown jacket and black hat, spoke with a gruff voice.

"I want the money here, and the damn safe opened, or by god I'll put enough holes yer bank teller to imitate Swiss cheese! Now your nice manager here will go to his office here and take care of that safe!"

The large man lifted Daley, who winced in pain as he is pushed toward his office, and Chris dropped his licorice and ran behind the large oak desk and scampered underneath it.

"Just do as he tells you, Jim!" one of the gunmen shouted behind him. Jim recognized that voice.

"C-Clancy! What have you gone and done, man!" Jim wanted to say more, but a hard shove from Daniels ended any conversation he could engage in. Jim was about to call out to Chris, but saw that he appeared to have left the office, somehow. Jim went over to the safe, just behind his desk, and almost started as he noticed Chris' hand sticking out from just under the desk. He turned quickly toward the safe, hoping that the gunman didn't see him notice Chris. He quickly but nervously turned the dials on the safe.

"I'll give you what you want, just take the money and go! We're good people here, we don't mean you any harm! Here, here it is!"

Jim was thrown aside as the gunman opened the safe wide and started bagging the money.

"I got the safe open, boys, let's get out of-"

Daniels had just started celebrating when he noticed the small hand just underneath the desk. He looked to Daley, who suddenly looked even more fearful as he followed Daniels' gaze to Chris. Daniels reached under the desk and pulled Chris from under the desk. Chris yelped as Daniels stood him up.

"Holy crap! So what do we have here? This your servant boy, Dandy? Maybe we'll take him for insurance!"

Jim tried to plead for Chris, but was only rewarded with gun butt to the head. He gripped his head in pain and stood up. He looked up just in time to see Chris kick Daniels in the leg, causing him to let go of Chris' collar. Chris bolted for the door, and Daniels raised his gun to fire, and Jim jumped for the gun, but was too late as Daniels' gun fired at Chris Tarver...

Chapter 5: The Force of Many

In which Jack and Miles Jepson find themselves in a vicious gunfight in an attempt to stop Daniels and Co.

Miles Jepson looked at the gun in awe. He had thought Sam would've had it buried with him, but was glad to see it again. Jack let Miles take his time with it. After all, it's like seeing an old friend again. Miles took his soot-covered gloves off, and set his hefty frame in his favorite chair in his smithy. He let his assistant Jesse finish that new wagon wheel for Buddy Reynolds, and inspected the gun, nodding with approval at the cleanliness of it. Miles looked up at Jack and smiled.

"This is a fantastic gun, if I do say so myself, Mr. Tarver."

"Call me Jack."

"Miles. I remember the day I modified this for Sam. Just days before he left to join the Union. The entire town was so proud of him. Him and Clancy Miller."

Jack perked up at this.

"Clancy? I don't remember meeting him."

Miles shrugged his shoulders as he handed the gun back to Jack.

"You may not have. Clancy left a little later, and got injured and was sent home, where he met Patricia. She sure healed him up pretty good back in those days, I tell you. They had a decent ranch going, 'till sickness claimed his entire herd, and then, well, you've probably been by his home. Shame about his little girl..."

Jack nodded his head. He was about to ask about the gun when he heard screams and yells coming from down the street. Jack and Miles walked quickly outside to see what was going on. He could see men and women running to and fro, toward and away from just down the street-near the bank. Jack grabbed the drunkard Tony Parker as he tried to run by.

"Tony! What's going on?"

"Hot damn, Jack! Some men have come and are robbin' the bank! I'm going to find the Marshal! My money's in there, dammit!"

Jack let go of Tony and began to run toward the bank, hoping that Chris had already left. While Jack ran toward the bank, Chris just narrowly dodged a bullet fired by Daniels. Chris could barely hear the gunshot his heart beat so loudly in his head.

Chris stopped dead in his tracks as one of the robbers stood between him and the door to freedom. He didn't-couldn't-bring himself to look back to see if Mr. Daley was all right. The robber in front of him gasped as he saw Chris.

"My god! Chris!"

Chris thought he could recognize the voice, and a confirmation from Daniels proved it.

"Grab or shoot the kid, Clancy!"

Chris froze in fear as he looked at Helen's father.

"M-Mr. Miller? Why are you doing this?"

Clancy pulled down his red bandana and pleaded with Chris as he forcefully but at the same time gently grabbed his arm and led him back.

"I'm doing this for Helen, can't you see? So she can get better!"

"Damn it, Clancy! I wouldn't have thought it would be you! What got into you, man?"

Clancy looked up at the voice, his expression changing to anger, if not outright hate as he saw Jim Daley being pushed into the room by Daniels. The other patrons lay on the ground, a few of the women, and even some of the men, whispered Clancy's name in disbelief. Clancy spat down at Jim's feet.

"The hell you know, Jim! I needed the money, and you turned your back on me, and Helen! You were at her baptism, man! How could a father not do this for his child!"

Jim shook his head.

"Aw, Clancy, I should have told you before. I've been-"

Jim was trying to tell Clancy some good news when one of the gunmen yelled as he looked out of the front window.

"Hey, there's a man with a gun just taking cover behind the wagon across the street!"

Jack cursed himself for not being sneakier as he checked his gun for ammunition. Miles followed right beside him with his shotgun. Jack looked at Miles, who looked afraid, but ready. Jack noticed other townsfolk, particularly two miners, just down the street with shotguns running toward the bank. Jack knew this was going to turn into a bloodbath very quickly if he didn't come up with a plan. Jack tried to peer into the bank, to see if he could see any signs of Chris, but a bullet bouncing off of the wagon stopped him from peering any further.

"Stay back! We got a whole lot of people here! Won't hesitate to put holes in 'em!"

Jack looked over at Miles, who already knew what Jack was thinking.

"No back way in, Jack. They have to come out the front. Can't believe this-this sort of things' never happened before! What with Elijah gone-what do we do?"

"Why ask me? What makes you think I know anything about this?"

"You were a soldier once."

"You do have a point. Give me a second to think."

Jack looked around for a moment, and nearly slapped himself for not seeing it earlier. He had to get those men out of the cover provided by the bank. It was a long shot, but there weren't any other options left. Jack motioned for the two miners down the street to come closer to hear his idea.

Chris found himself sitting next to Jack Daley, who was still nursing the bruise on the back of his head since Daniels hit him earlier. They heard Jack call out to them, and Chris nearly answered, but stopped himself. He looked toward the old woman Matilda, a foot away from him, who stared at the ground in fear. Two of the robbers kept watch outside, while the others were embroiled in an argument about what to do next.

"That's just great, Daniels! So what do we do now? The townsfolk out there will gun us down the moment we try to leave! We could take hostages, but they'll slow us down!" said Swenson, noticeably fearful. Clancy didn't speak, but looked dead at Chris and Mr. Daley the entire time.

"Dammit Swenson, don't lose your nerve. They're just townsfolk, they can't stop us! We can take a few folk and get rid of them once we clear town."

Daniels was about to say more when Jack interrupted him.

"You better give up, or we'll burn you out! If you give up now, we promise you a fair trial!"

Daniels snorted at this, but he was stunned by what he heard next.

"Jack! We got your boy, but he's okay! We just want to get out of town!"

Jack couldn't believe his ears.

"Clancy? Jesus, man, how did you-never mind! Send those people out! We can't let you leave with the money! Think of Patricia and Helen!"

"I do, Jack, every day!"

Daniels grabbed Clancy by his collar, and shoved him back away from the door. Fool was about to do them all in.

"The hell you think your doin', Clancy? Getting cold feet? We're past that point, man! If we're caught it's the noose for us! Now, we get the boy..."

Both men jumped as the windows all around them exploded with glass as several rocks shattered them, and gusts of smoke filled the room like a tidal wave.

"Those crazy fools set fire to us! We gotta go!"

Two of the men ran out of building in a panic, following Ned Harris and his kids as they scrambled out. Jack saw the two men as they evacuated and yelled for them to stop. He was never sure why men like that seemed to think they could take a shot in open space, but they shot at Jack, hitting the wagon, and Jack raised his gun faster than lightening and shot the first man, who didn't have a chance to fire again as his body windmilled to the ground. The second man, Swenson, tried to shoot at Miner Tom, who was using a carpet just around the corner to send the smoke created from the brush they set near the side of the bank right through the window, but Miles shot the second man in the leg, and he promptly dropped his gun as he clutched his leg in pain. Things were starting to happen too fast for Bryce Daniels. He coughed through the haze of smoke as he saw that damn coward Clancy trying to usher Chris and Jim Daley out of the bank.

"Clancy, what the hell are you doing?"

"We gotta get out of here, Bryce! It's finished!"

"The hell it is! Get that boy and the banker back here NOW!"

Clancy pushed Chris and Daley out of the door as Daniels raised his gun.

"G-Go, Chris!"

Clancy tried to shoot at Daniels, but was too slow as Daniels reeled off the shot first, and Clancy crumpled down at the door, but not before taking one last shot that felled Daniels.

Jack saw Chris and Jim run from the bank, the smoke starting to obscure even his vision, and saw Chris turn back, yelling Clancy's name as two gunshots rang out. Just as he did, the two remaining robbers emerged, one firing his gun at Daley, just missing him as he tried to run back to Chris, and the other man was about to fire when Jack reeled off two quick shots from his gun, sending both men sprawling to the ground. Jack waved for the miners to stop moving the smoke, and slowly walked around the wagon toward the bank, as Mr. Daley did the same, clutching his shoulder. Jack walked forward cautiously, and didn't notice that one of the men, Swenson, was still alive, and waited for Jack to pass him, and raised his gun and pointed it at Jack's back. He let out a curse at Jack and cocked his gun. Jack heard the gun, and twirled around to face the sound, but knew he would be too late. A shot rang out, and Swenson cried out in pain before collapsing on the ground. Jack looked at Swenson's lifeless body, and then toward the saloon, where Blackjack was holstering his gun, leaning against the saloon post. He tipped his hat at Jack, and walked back into the saloon. Doc Harrison chose this moment to run from the saloon, where he and many men watched the action unfold, toward the bank, clutching his medical bag. Jack couldn't see Chris through the smoke, and took a chance. There could still be more men in there.

"Chris! Chris! Answer me, son!"

As he walked closer, the smoke was starting to clear, and he could hear Chris sobbing as he approached, with Mr. Daley just behind him. Doc Harrison tried to hold Daley to check him, but Daley waved him off. Jack saw Chris kneeling over Clancy Miller. One look inside the bank at the crumpled body of Daniels told Jack everything he needed to know. Chris clutched Clancy's hand as Doc Harrison checked him. After a few seconds, Doc Harrison looked at Chris and sadly shook his head. Daley knelt beside Chris and looked at Clancy, tears welling in his eyes. Clancy couldn't speak, but his eyes met Daley's.

"You didn't have to do this, Clancy! I tried to tell you, an uncle of mine died recently, and he left me his land. I was just able to sell the land last week, and I already ordered the medicine for Helen!"

Chris looked up to meet Daley's tear-filled eyes as Clancy did the same, his face lighting up, telling Jim that he understood.

"Helen's going to live, Clancy. She'll live a long life, man!"

Clancy smiled as he heard the words, and then died. Doc Harrison closed Clancy's eyes, and looked up toward those who stood there.

"Someone has to tell Patricia and Helen."

Jack was about to volunteer when Marshal Bronson stepped forward, just having arrived, looking bewildered as he surveyed the aftermath of the failed bank robbery.

"I'll do it, Doc, as soon as someone explains what the hell happened. I'll look for you to do that, Jack, after you get your boy home."

Jack knew that Elijah wasn't asking. He pried Chris away from Clancy's body, and walked Chris toward their wagon. He could feel the townspeople's eyes on them, and was slightly surprised to feel the pats on the back as he loaded Chris into the wagon. He didn't speak, and Chris refused to. The wagon ride home was a silent one, as was Chris as soon as they arrived. Jack told Chris to stay at home, and not to bother with chores for the day. Chris nodded his head and went to his room. Jack unhitched the wagon and rode his horse back to town. He didn't want to leave Chris, but he had to deal with Marshal Bronson first. He passed by the Miller stead, and sadly looked at it as he rode by. He stopped after a few feet, and rode right up to the home, and knocked on the door. Patricia answered the door, and invited Jack in, but he politely refused, taking off his hat, and telling her one of the most painful things he's ever had to tell anyone. Patricia almost fainted with grief as she heard the words that her dear Clancy was gone, and Jack had to hold her up, and gently helped her into the house, and decided that the Marshal's explanation would have to wait. There was some explaining –and consolation-that had to happen here first...

Chapter 6: Ellie and Helen

In which Jack meets the owner of the Stanton ranch, and the town begins to heal, but Chris notices that Helen is showing signs that things are not as well as they think...

It had been a relatively easy day for Doctor Howard Harrison. The children had started school just a few days ago, and there hadn't been any incidents since the Bank robbery, now a month old. "Doc" Harrison found himself riding on a fine September day back toward the town, just after delivering the newest edition to the Steward family, a nine-pound baby boy they named Colt. Doc almost laughed at that. The silly things parents would name their children! The town was a bustle as usual, but peaceful. Not even a stitch from a bar brawl to contend with. Doc arrived at his office as dismounted his horse, and took off his saddlebags containing his field medical bag. He was about to step into his office when he noticed Patricia Miller walking by. She looked tired and unhappy, but how else could she feel after losing her husband to a gunfight that he brought upon himself. Doc tipped his hat to her.

"Mrs. Miller. Good day to you!"

She walked by him, and he wasn't even sure if she noticed the gesture, staring straight ahead with sad brown eyes and bags under her eyes that spoke of days without proper sleep. He shook his head, wishing that he could do more. He stepped inside his office and tried to sit down, but after a few moments felt restless, and grabbed his hat as he exited. He made his way to the saloon, where he was surprised to find Jack there, hat off, drinking some sort of clear liquid at the bar. He noticed that Blackjack was dealing cards at his usual table, making a couple of men all the poorer.

"Jack, how are you, man! A little early in the day to be drinking, eh?"

Jack held up his drink and smiled.

"Water, Doc, just water. I'm meeting with the owner of the Stanton Ranch to see about buying some horses for breeding. What are you doing here? Slow day?"

Doc took that as an invitation, and ordered water and sat in the barstool next to Jack. Harvey the bartender was all too happy to oblige.

"Yes, I suppose so. So I take it you have the ranch ready?"

"Yeah, except for one fence post I need to replace, but that's a small matter."

"I've been meaning to ask you, did you and Sam see much action in the war?"

"Not as much as you might think. By the time we joined the war was nearly over. It was mostly going house to house, checking for leftover enemy soldiers who either didn't know-or didn't care-that the war was over, but what little we did see..."

Jack trailed off, lost in his own memories that cleared when Doc asked another question.

"So was Sam a good soldier?"

Jack looked at Doc, and noticed something different about his demeanor. He couldn't quite put his finger on it, but this wasn't the first time the doctor had asked.

"He was a great scout. The best of the company, and certainly of Fort Smith. Could spot the enemy a mile away. He kind of had a feeling for them, rather than seeing them. Either way, he was great." Jack said, looking hard at the doctor, who looked rather relieved.

"He was good. Thank you for that, Jack. Thank you."

Jack looked around once more to make sure his party hadn't arrived yet, and asked the question he'd been dying to ask.

"Why do you ask so many questions about Sam? Are you related to him somehow?"

Doc Harrison loosened the collar of his white shirt and motioned for Jack to follow him to a table away from the other patrons, and waited for Jack to sit down.

"Years ago, I hate to say this, but when I was a young man, just married and full of spunk, I found myself walking by the river one slow Saturday afternoon, and ran across Meryl Spivey. Actually she was Meryl Jackson before, but Paul Spivey had already been courting her. Well, one thing led to another, and well, you know..."

He trailed off, but Jack knew exactly what had happened.

"So your Sam's real father?"

"Yes."

"And the knowledge of that-"

"Even today, the Spivey's are well regarded around here, and the knowledge of what I've done will cause people to distrust me!"

Jack sipped his water as he thought about this, and agreed, it would damage him, and the men in town would never trust Doc with anything more than treating a light bruise, especially if it involves their wives, and even though Doc's wife Mabel was years dead, some of her family were still living in town.

"I know I asked, but why tell me?"

"Because you're a good man, Jack. I've seen you around town. 'The Great Negro Negotiator' they're starting to call you. You've dispelled quite a few arguments, stopped fights before they begin, and I know you don't pass judgment. I think that's why Sam liked you so much, and I was never able to tell Sam, though I wanted to, so I guess since he's gone I figured you're the next best person."

Jack sipped his drink, trying to understand *why* Doc would tell him such a thing and promptly stopped, as did Doc Harrison, as they witnessed the beauty that walked up to their table. Even Blackjack stopped a moment before returning his gaze to the game at hand. She was a long red-haired woman, wearing riding leathers, somewhat expensive, looking custom made. She had on brown pants and slightly darker brown boots, and a blue shirt. She had piercing brown eyes that locked on Jack and Doc Harrison. She gave a wide smile as she spoke.

"You Jack Tarver?"

Jack stood up, a little confused. Doc Harrison stood up as well.

"Yes I am. And who might you be?"

"Ellie Stanton. I'm here to sell you those horses, Mr. Tarver. My father was supposed to come, but took ill. He sends his apologies. I hope this doesn't inconvenience you."

"Um, no, no, not at all, Miss Stanton!" Jack said, stumbling through his words.

"Call me Ellie, Jack."

Blackjack tried to smile at Ellie from across the bar, but she shot him a dirty look, prompting him to return quickly to the intricacies of poker. She-and her father-must still be angry about that ranch hand he killed a month ago.

Jack invited Ellie to sit down, and Doc Harrison excused himself from the table and left the saloon. He was far too old for this game, and knew it was time to leave the youngsters to themselves. Doc Harrison walked outside and took a deep breath and walked leisurely down the street, narrowly avoiding Chris Tarver running by with the Peacock Brothers.

"C'mon, keep up, Manny! Old man Smythe could outrun you!"

Chris laughed as he finally escaped the first week of school. School marm Nancy Carroll wasn't as much of a troll as the other kids said, but not by much. He was happy to get out, and make his way to the general store before heading home to do his homework for the day. Manny Peacock, a slightly rotund boy, raced with Chris but his skinny brother Alex suddenly stopped, looking toward the center of the busy street.

"Hey! Look at that! Isn't that Helen Miller?"

Chris and Manny stopped running as they looked at Helen, who stared unemotionally toward the end of the street, where the stage was just coming toward them. They were surprised to see her, since no one had seen her since her father's death. She never emerged from the house, even after a total recovery, and never came to town, or anywhere else. No one could blame her, losing her father like that. Chris had tried to come over to her house several times, but was turned away with an apology by Mrs. Miller. Chris started to walk slowly to her, and his eyes followed her to the oncoming stage, which picked up speed. He noticed that she kept walking toward the center of the street-and the stage! Chris started to run toward her, at the same time that the stage driver noticed that no, the little girl ahead of him had no intention of stopping. Mr. Miller emerged from the bank and dropped the groceries she had just bought.

"Oh my god! Helen! Get out of the street! Helen!"

The driver tried to stop, but knew he would be too late. Chris found himself running, without even thinking, right at Helen. Jack and Ellie ran from the saloon, and Jack yelled Chris' name, but he didn't hear him. All Chris could think about was Helen. Helen didn't seem to notice anything except the oncoming stage, so she never saw Chris right before he tackled her to the ground, the momentum carrying them both just beyond the wheels of the stage as it skidded to a stop-several feet from where they stood. Chris looked up, amazed at what he did. It wasn't long before what seemed to be the entire town came upon them. Helen never looked up, never even responded. Chris did notice that a single tear rolled down her right cheek, but didn't have long to think about it when Jack knelt beside him and gripped his arm, and Helen found herself in her mothers' arms. Jack began to look Chris over.

"You all right, son?"

"I'm okay, Pa! It's nothing!"

The stagehand had already jumped off the stage and spoke to anyone within the sound of his voice.

"Nothing? That was a whole lot of nothing, boy! You saved this girl here! You're a hero!"

Various people chimed the affirmative, and Jack lifted Chris, who smiled as much as he could as he looked over at Helen, who was being checked over by a frightened Mrs. Miller, and Doc Harrison was there too, looking her over. Ellie walked over and shook Chris' hand.

"That was a brave thing you did for her, Mr. Tarver. I see saving people runs in the family."

Chris tried to smile at her and looked back at Helen, but somehow, she and her mother were gone...

Burt James sat somberly in the Pine Valley Saloon in Kansas City, nursing his last whiskey. He had been traveling with a new group of no goods for the last several months, and made a little money, but not as much as he'd hoped, at least not for the people he had to kill. He looked toward the bartender just down the bar serving two other men, one of which was reading a newspaper to the other. He waved at the bartender, who nodded his head. Burt went back to staring into his glass as he heard something that brought him back to life.

"Oh, look at this, Harvey. There was an attempted bank robbery in Liberty a few weeks ago."

"Really? I got a cousin who lives there. Anyone hurt?"

"Just the robbers. All but one was killed, and get this, not by the Marshal, but by one of the townsfolk!"

"That's funny, so who is he?"

"Let's see...here it is. Jack Tarver was the man who did them in. If he weren't a Negro they probably woulda' made him sheriff!"

Both men laughed, and didn't notice Burt James ran out yelling Jack Tarver's name in joy. He had to find Jeremy Davis and let him know that he was right!

They found Tarver!

Chris found himself skipping rocks across the creek not far from the house, waiting for the Peacock brothers to show up. It was a beautiful Saturday afternoon, and he had just finished helping Pa mend a fence on the west side of the ranch. He skipped another rock and counted the skips when Helen suddenly appeared beside him. Chris nearly jumped out of his skin.

"Helen! Where did you come from?"

Helen didn't answer for a moment, just staring at the creek, and then shrugged her shoulders.

"From home, where else? So what are you doing here?"

"Just skippin' rocks, waitin' for the Peacock brothers. You?"

Chris thought that he saw a smile on Helen's face. It lasted a moment, but was a welcome sight to see.

"I just wanted to thank you for saving my life a few days ago. I don't know what got into me. I just thought about Pa, and how what happened was my fault. No one blames me, but I know it was. Even the way mother looks at me some times."

Chris and Helen both picked up rocks and started to throw them. Chris wasn't used to playing with a girl, but at the moment didn't mind at all.

"Your Pa did the wrong thing, trying to rob the bank, but he saved me when it counted. That shows what kind of man he was. It wasn't anyone's fault, and heck, I don't even blame him, and you sure shouldn't blame yourself."

"Why are you and your Pa such good folk, Chris? I've lived here my whole life, and while I've met a bunch of people, even colored people, you two are so different from just about anyone. The whole town talks about you."

Chris skipped another rock in silence. Yes, he had heard the word spreading about what his father had done, and knew, better than anyone, that he took no pleasure in it, and refused to talk about it. He warned Chris that he did what he did because he had no choice, that if there had been another way he would have done it. Chris threw his last stone. It skipped the creek seven times, the most he'd ever done.

"Good throw! Betcha I can do better!"

Helen was about to rear up and throw when some shouts interrupted them. They turned to find the Peacock Brothers coming near them.

"Look at that! Chris Tarver's playin' with Crazy Helen! You jump in front of any wagons lately?" said Manny, while Alex laughed.

Helen tried to fight back the tears, and looked to Chris. Surely he would defend her. Of course he would! Chris looked at Helen and then to the boys.

"She isn't crazy, Manny! You stop calling her that."

Manny looked to Alex and smiled.

"We wuz just kiddin' around, Helen! Your Pa saved my Pa from a mountain lion a few years back. Wanna play with us? We were about to head up to old man Harvey's place. They say there's ghosts up there."

Helen smiled and nodded her head. Chris was a little surprised.

"I didn't think girls like that sort of thing!"

Helen started walking toward the Peacock Brothers and smiled.

"I ain't a regular girl, Chris Tarver!"

With that, the group set off for Harvey's Hill.

Chapter 7: Ellie

In which Jack Tarver gets to know Ellie and her father, who may be in more trouble than they let on...

Jack checked himself in the mirror again. He almost wanted to ask Chris about it, if he looked nice, but Chris had gone with some friends to Harvey's Hill. Jack had already gotten word that it was an abandoned house, but they would find little trouble there. Jack was almost relieved that Chris was away. He wasn't sure how Chris would view the dinner with Ellie and her father. Jack wasn't looking to get married again, though he wouldn't be opposed to it. Certainly Elizabeth wouldn't want him to be alone forever. Ellie seemed to be a nice woman, so what would the hurt be? Jack figured he would tell Chris later, if things moved forward. Of course, Jack and Ellie had been seeing each other for the last several weeks, so maybe it was time to let Chris know (though Jack was sure a smart boy like Chris had already figured it out). Jack smiled to himself as he saddled his horse. Such a smart boy he and Elizabeth brought into the world. Elizabeth was a white woman, and they were able to live outside of town, but Ellie was well known around *this* town. Most folks knew they were seeing each other but if there were objections, and Jack was sure there were, they didn't say it in public. He began to ride out, and an hour later found himself entering the Stanton Ranch. It was a large ranch, and Jack noticed that the fencing wasn't kept up very well. The house itself sat on top of a hill, a brown and red two-story home that had fancy curtains hanging from the windows that even Jack had to notice. The flowers around the home were worn and looked as if it hadn't been taken care of, and some of the wood on the house itself seemed to be rotting away. He entered the fence, and rode up the small hill. Normally it would take quite a few men to maintain such a large spread, and Jack was surprised to find only two ranch hands on the property from what he could see. Of course, there had been three until Blackjack was forced to kill one of them two months ago. He tipped his hat as he rode by them, and neither man responded, looking dirty and a little angry. Jack arrived at the house as Ellie ran out to meet him, wearing a white shirt and gray riding pants, her red hair glistening in the sun. She smiled that smile that could brighten the darkest cave as Jack dismounted his horse.

"Jack, it's good to see you. Come inside and meet my father!"

Ellie called for one of the hands to take care of Jack's horse, and held his hand as they entered the home. Despite what the outside looked like, the inside was a beautiful and pristine home, full of flowers and family pictures. The floors were made of a wood Jack wasn't familiar with, but it was shiny, with a large Mexican rug covering the living room area. Jack was almost afraid to bump into anything as he looked around. Ellie must have noticed his curiosity about the place, because she was silent for a moment as well, smiling at Jack, and then a deep booming Scottish voice hammered through the silence.

"So this must be the hero Jack Tarver! Welcome to my home!"

A burly yet short gentleman walked into the room, with the help of a black cane. Archer Stanton wore a gray gentleman's coat, and a purple vest underneath that. Despite the cane, Archer walked with the air of a nobleman. He wore thin- rimmed glasses, and sported a gray handlebar moustache; His green eyes were weathered with adventures Jack could only guess at. He grabbed Jack's hand and shook it. Jack was surprised at the man's strength, and Archer noticed.

"Thought I'd be a frail thing, eh? There's more behind the cover of *this* book, Mr. Jack! Kind of like yourself! Archer Stanton, at your service!"

Jack smiled as he regarded Archer.

"Pleasure's mine, Mr. Stanton."

"Call me Archie! Everyone else does! Sit down, Jack, sit down. Consuela! Some wine for our guest, please!" said Archie, clapping his hands twice as he, with Ellie's help, sat down in an elegant, yet worn, red velvet chair. As if on queue, a dainty but pretty Mexican girl, with her long hair tied in pigtails, walked in and stood before them as they sat down. She held a tray with three ornate looking glasses, and a glass decanter of wine.

Archie looked at the young woman longingly, but quickly as he gestured toward Jack.

"Serve our guest first, Consuela. Jack, this wine is straight from the vineyards of Italy!"

Jack took the glass, thanking Consuela, and took a sip. It wasn't really for him, but he smiled at his gracious host regardless.

"It's good stuff, Archie. It tastes expensive. How did you get it?"

"Ah! One has to know the right people. Trade ship from Italy, used to know her captain, comes to port in San Francisco twice a year. I have a man wait for him, and then the rest is history."

Jack took another sip and suddenly felt the eyes of both Archie and Ellie on him, and he shifted in his seat uncomfortably. They smiled at him in silence. Like the look before a wild animal pounces.

"So, Archie, the price for the horses was quite—well, cheaper than I thought."

Ellie looked to her father, almost worriedly. Archie waved Jack off.

"Let's call it neighborly hospitality. Especially after saving my money from those bank robbers. My little thank you. Mine and Ellie's."

Consuela returned to the room and announced that dinner was ready. Jack breathed a sigh of relief. What Archie said next soon dispelled that.

"Let's go eat, Jack, and let's discuss you joining our family!"

Two hours and some steaks later found Jack walking up a hill just behind the house with Ellie. The sun had already vanished to show a brilliant moon. Jack wondered about Chris for a moment, and was sure that Chris had gotten home when he was supposed to.

Ellie put her arm through Jack's as they walked.

"Jack, you've been very quiet. Is everything all right?"

Jack looked toward the night sky for a moment.

"Fine, Ellie, it's fine. Your father is a good man. He's taken great care of you, despite losing his wife so many years ago."

"I admit it's been hard, but you're doing the same thing with Chris. It's not easy, but then again I don't think it's supposed to be. Of course, with a woman around the house..."

Jack stopped walking, and turned to face Ellie. The moonlight lit her beautiful face and highlighted her red hair. She smiled, which made what Jack said even harder than it had to be.

"You're a good woman, Ellie, you really are. But I'm not so sure I want this just yet. We need to take this slower, at least for a little while. Can you do that?"

The smile disappeared for a moment from Ellie's face as she regarded the question, and then lit up again as she looked up at him. Jack looked into her eyes, and wondered if he was being crazy or simply stupid. Chris does need a mother, to give him the things he couldn't, but still...Jack drew Ellie closer.

"We can take as much time as you need, Jack Tarver. We have all the time in the world."

With that Jack kissed her, and she seemed to melt the moment their lips touched. They drew even closer, and the world seemed to disappear around them. They didn't notice that Archie was looking at them through the window of his bedroom, smiling to himself, and hoped that his-and Ellie's- problems would soon be over. Negro or not, thank goodness for Jack Tarver.

Archie made his way back downstairs as he heard the door close an hour later as Ellie walked back in. Archie was so excited he could barely contain himself.

Ellie walked toward him, saying nothing. He motioned her forward.

"So it went well, yes?"

"He wants to take it slow."

Archie winced at this, but took comfort that at least there's still a chance.

"Slow? What's he waiting for?"

"He just wants to make sure, that's all. He does have a boy to think about. We should give him the time he needs!"

Archie looked at her for a moment, before slapping her hard across the face. Ellie twirled around and fell to the floor and looked up, holding her bruised cheek as a furious Archie stood over her. His eyes flashed with controlled fury.

"Damn you, girl! We're standin' at the end, you get me? First that slimy gambler killed Miguel, and before long those Russians in New York will come calling! If we don't have that money we lose everything! Everything! You think Tarver will take you then? Hmm?"

Ellie wiped a tear from her face and stood up, her hard stare reminding Archie that she was still his daughter, strength and all.

"I know that, daddy! A man like Tarver has to be treated with care, with a light touch, not with a club! Tarver has the money we need! If we take it slowly, he'll give it to us because of his feelings for me!"

Archie moved to his velvet chair and sat down. He began to calm down.

"Are you sure he has feelings for you?"

Ellie started up the stairs, her cheek still stinging from that slap. It had surprised her, as it was something her father had never done before. He was starting to be consumed with his problems, and even took to drinking more than he ever had before, and Ellie knew she had to succeed more than ever before she lost him entirely.

"I kissed him, didn't I? No man, white, black or other has ever resisted me, and I know he wants me, and soon, we'll all have everything we want. Hell, you'll be able to settle things with that gambler, too."

With that Ellie stormed up the stairs, leaving Archer to his thoughts, and he slumped over in his seat and laid his head in his hands. He had never hit Ellie in her life, and he felt horrible about that, but Archer had never asked Ellie to sacrifice so much of herself, but he was determined to make sure she lived a long and rich life, even if he had to kill for it in the end. His trip to Hell would be worth that...

Patricia Miller set down feed for the few cows they had left and started walking back toward the house. Usually this would be something for Helen to do, but she begged her mother to let her go to the Tarver home. She smiled a little to herself. Chris was a good boy, and would grow to be a good man, and who knows? Perhaps the world will change enough for them to be more? Patricia looked up just in time to see a lone rider coming up the dirt road. She waved at the rider as he dismounted and approached her. The dark bearded man tipped his hat.

"Hello, ma'am, I'm sorry to disturb you, but I'm new to these parts. I was hopin' you could help me look for someone."

"I'd be happy to. Who are you lookin' for?"

"Man by the name of Jack Tarver. Y'see, I'm his brother, and I came to visit, see how he's getting along."

Patricia smiled at the gentleman. Finally the Tarvers get some other family out here!

"Oh yes! They live just a mile up this road, just over that hill. Tell Jack I said hello!"

"Thank you kindly, ma'am, I will. You bet I will."

Patricia watched as the man rode away and up the road toward the Tarver home. Little did she know that Godfrey wasn't going there. Not just yet. Some folks need to know that he's found Jack's spread...

Jack rode up to the house slowly, and noticed that it didn't look as if Chris were home. Jack rode toward the stables, and noticed that Chris' horse wasn't there. Jack rode straight back to the house and walked inside the house, and noticed that it hadn't looked like Chris had ever come back. Jack shook his head, and jumped back on his horse. Now Jack was worried. Jack jumped back on his horse and rode for Harvey's Hill, not noticing Godfrey down the road. Godfrey noticed him, however, and smiled. Tomorrow was going to be a fun day. A fun day indeed.

Chapter 8: Harvey's Hill

In which Chris and his friends go for a little adventure, and find more than they bargained for...

Alex Peacock looked over at his brother Manny, who looked back at him and shrugged his shoulders, and looked to Chris and Helen, both of whom looked mischievously back at them. Alex returned his gaze to the large two story home before them. The house was dank and dark, and they could see the spider webs and vines practically covering the house like a transparent skin. Everyone stood deathly still. They had all heard the story of old man Harvey. It seemed that about thirty years ago he went crazy and killed his wife and two boys, and then hung himself, but not before cursing the people of Liberty. Helen was the first to break from the spell of fear the house had woven, and ran up to the door.

"C'mon, boys! Let's see what's inside! Maybe Harvey's ghost!"

Helen then opened the door. Chris smiled and followed after her, as did the Peacock brothers, because they weren't going to be outdone by a girl. They followed in and stepped through the door, the rotting floorboards creaking as they moved into the living room. There was a table with three chairs, and a fourth that was broken. It was getting close to evening, but they could see that there was a hole in the roof, that went through the second floor all the way to the bottom, sending light into the center of the living room. They moved around the light, almost afraid to step into it, and Helen saw a candle by the fireplace. She motioned silently to it, and Alex fished inside his denim overalls and found the flint and tinder. He walked over to the candle and set it down, and started trying to get a spark. Chris and Manny went into the kitchen and looked around. They saw a knife sitting on a small table.

"Hey Chris, look at that! I think that was the knife old man Harvey used to kill his sons! Don't touch it, though! His ghost won't like that..."

Chris started to pick up the knife, but a wince from Manny made him think twice. They heard a whoop from the living room as Alex finally lit the candle. Helen placed it in the web-covered candleholder, and the two of them started their way upstairs slowly as Chris and Manny continued to look around the kitchen and dining room. Harvey must have been rich, due to the extravagance of the candleholders and paintings that even extremely damaged and dirty looked expensive.

"Why did Harvey go crazy, Manny?"

"No one knows, really. My Pa told me that they think Harvey's wife was bedin' wit another man, and Harvey found out and went mad. But everyone has their own thinkin' about it."

Chris looked around and they heard Helen scream from upstairs. Both boys ran up the stairs, and Manny yelped as his foot fell through stair that suddenly broken under him. He carefully fished his foot out and continued to follow Chris up the stairs, only to find Chris and Alex laughing at Helen, who looked upset as she stood in what used to be a childs' bedroom, now nothing more than broken wood planks in the floor and cobwebs everywhere, and a dusty unkempt bed covered with spiders, bugs, and rotten yellow sheets.

"It seems Helen here thought she saw someone move under the sheet! It was a breeze movin' the sheet!" Alex said, between giggles.

"Stop laughin' at me, Alex Peacock!" Helen grabbed the sheet and threw it on Alex, who yelled in surprise.

"Awmugod! There's spiders! Get me out!"

Manny and Chris helped a yelling Alex out of the sheet as it was Helen's turn to laugh, which came to an abrupt end as she looked at them.

"Did you hear that?"

Manny scoffed at Helen.

"Stop playin, I ain't heard nothin.'"

Chris stopped moving as well as he pulled the last of the sheet off of Alex.

"She's right! I hear it too!"

Alex brushed a spider off of him.

"Sounds like it's coming from outside!"

They moved to a window and looked out, and saw five men dismount from their horses. They took off their saddlebags and walked into the house.

Alex crouched down, and everyone else followed suit.

"Ain't supposed to be anyone here! Wonder who they are?"

Helen started walking carefully back toward the stairs.

"Let's find out!" she whispered. Chris followed after her, and Manny and Alex behind him. She knelt at the top of the stairwell as the men entered in a commotion, throwing their leather bags down everywhere. They couldn't really see the men, but could hear them just fine, and this is what they heard:

"Thank god we're here at last! Think we rode long enough?"

"Stop yer bellyachin'. We're here, ain't we?"

"Yeah, yeah, so where's Godfrey?"

"Rode ahead a day ago, to find the man's spread."

"So you think he's got the money?"

"Maybe. He's supposed to have a big spread around here. I think he's got a kid. Daughter, I think. I forgot what Jeremy said."

Helen looked to Chris, who shrugged his shoulders. They had no idea who they were talking about, or even who this Godfrey was.

Manny and Alex looked at each other, worry etching itself across their faces. Alex slowly backed away and walked down the hall as quietly as possible as the others continued to eavesdrop.

"I hope he still has that gold. If he don't..."

"No man would give up that much gold. Folks say he's got a ranch out hereabouts. Maybe the gold is on his property. Probably bought with it."

Chris and Helen were listening so intently they didn't notice that something was bothering Manny. Perhaps it was the dust in the air, or perhaps an allergy of some sort, but Manny felt the sneeze coming a split second before it happened. He raised his hand quickly to quiet it, but wasn't fast enough!

Ah-choo!

"What the hell wuz that?"

Manny rose up quickly, and his face was a strange mixture of terror and apology, but Helen and Chris never saw it as they leapt to their feet as if shot from a cannon and bolted down the hall even as they heard footsteps coming quickly up the stairs. They ran into the farthest bedroom, appearing to have once been a boys' room. Helen and Chris jumped behind the bed, and Manny stopped on the other and looked quickly around for Alex, and the plodding footsteps reached the top of the stair, and they heard a grizzled voice speak.

"Hey! There's someone here! Whoever you are, come out here!"

Chris and Helen found themselves holding hands in a vice grip no amount of metal could break, and they both shook with fear. As they heard the footsteps on the rotting wood grow closer, they heard Alex call them.

"Hey! Jump down here!"

Manny ran to the window and laughed before jumping out. Chris ran to the window and looked out and held out his hand for Helen. Helen ran and grabbed his hand. It seems that someone had decided to build a room downstairs, and extended the downstairs roof. Manny had already jumped down to the second roof and was climbing down the side of the building. Chris jumped out first and turned around to help Helen out. Helen never bothered to accept his hand, and was just pulling her leg out as a large hand grabbed her leg! Helen screamed, and Chris looked quickly around and saw a piece of wood that had broken away from the rotted sill, and had a sharp edge. Chris picked up the wood and stabbed the sharp end on the hand, and a spurt of blood shot out from the hand as the owner yelped in pain, letting go of Helen. She pulled away and ran to the edge of the roof where Manny and Alex were waiting for them. Chris and Helen jumped down together, and Manny and Alex did their best to catch them, but they all wound up in the dirt together. They got up and ran down a small ravine leading down to a creek behind the house. Manny and Alex ran until they finally stopped, and started laughing in between gasps for air. Chris started laughing too. Helen looked at them in awe. It was simply amazing what boys will laugh at! She shook her head and checked to see where they were. She recognized the creek as it was nearing the main road toward their homes. She started walking toward the dirt road, caked in dirt. The boys followed shortly behind her, giggling as they went. Helen turned her head and shot them a look, which made them laugh out loud. They soon stopped as a familiar voice cut through the darkness ahead of them.

"Chris? Is that you?"

"Over here, Pa!"

Chris ran forward, and met Jack sitting on his horse by the side of the road by the creek. Chris couldn't see his father's face in the darkness, and he didn't have to. He knew he was in trouble.

"I see we have Liberty's finest here. The Peacock Brothers, Helen Miller, and you. It's good to see you out and about, Helen. As for you, Chris, boy didn't I tell you to be home before dark?"

Chris looked down, unsure how to explain what had happened. He nodded his head silently. Jack shook his head and looked at the others, and even in moonlight could tell they were caked head to toe in mud. They all looked down and, like Chris, knew they were in trouble when they got home. Jack looked to the entire group.

"So where have you all been?"

Alex stepped forward to volunteer an answer.

"We wuz at Harvey's Hill, sir."

"And what were you doing there? I thought that house was abandoned."

"It is, sir. We were lookin' for ghosts."

Jack smiled at this and directed his next question to Chris.

"So did you find any?"

"No, sir. Um, we didn't find anything there at all." Chris lied. No point in telling him about those men.

Jack eyed his son critically. Chris was never given to lying before, and Jack decided to trust him now.

"We'll discuss *your* punishment tomorrow, son. I suppose I'll have to be the escort here. Let's go, kids. Your folks must be worried half to death!"

With that they left, and Chris hated lying to his father, little knowing that lie just saved Jack's life.

Chapter 9: Stanton's Game

In which Blackjack comes face to face with Archer Stanton at last, and finds himself in the one place he least expected to be...

"Call it."

Blackjack looked down at his cards, and his eyes darted around the Old Yellow saloon, as the evening began to bring out his favorite targets: miners drunk on success-or failure, and have come to drown their sorrows, and either way will either spend their hard earned money or try to make some the easy way at the card tables. Either way, Blackjack looked to make good. Blackjack smiled as he always did and turned his cards over.

"Straight flush." said the dealer.

His opponent across from him, an older, ragged cowboy taking a break before heading out, cursed under his breath as he threw his cards down in disgust.

"A pair. Blackjack wins."

The cowboy, still upset, tipped his hat at Blackjack and withdrew from the table, grabbing his saddle and heading for parts unknown. Blackjack smiled in satisfaction as he began to reach for his winnings. A polished wooden cane gently landed on the money, just barely missing Blackjack's hand. He looked up to see who would dare stop him, and smiled as he looked at the owner of the cane, which hid the cold chill that went down his spine.

"Archer Stanton. I thought you didn't get out much, seein' as how you have your darling daughter takin' care of your business."

"True, but I'll come out when I have personal business to take care of. Like you, for instance."

"Me? Whatever do you mean, Mr. Stanton? Big rancher man like yourself, I can't see what you'd need with a gambler."

"Don't bait me, Blackjack, or whatever name you've chosen to go by here, Alan Gentry. Yes, I've heard of you. I've even heard about the incident at Carson City. What was that? A child was killed in that little scuffle you had over a measly ten dollars!"

Blackjack bristled and quickly took stock of where Stanton's men were. He looked for the cleanest looking cowboys in the room, as surely they would reflect Stanton himself, and sure enough there were three of them, one standing at the bar ten feet away, his dark gaze never averting from Blackjack as his yellowed teeth chewed on a straw of barley, and another man stood to his right, leaning on the piano as the piano man kept playing his tunes, unaware of what was going on around him. Blackjack looked back at Archer and smiled. Archer smiled too.

"Well, Mr. Stanton, there's been many stories told of that day, and you know how stories can be. Like the ones of your ranch going broke. I mean, really, Archer, I see Ellie chasing around Jack Tarver like she can smell the money on him. You whoring her out, too?"

Now it was Stanton's turn to bristle. His hands shook in anger, and he stood up, barely able to contain his hatred. He removed his cane from the money on the table. He nodded at his men and they began to head for the doors.

"You killed my man, and Ellie's childhood friend. I won't forget that, Mr. Gentry. Enjoy your winnings while you can."

Stanton turned and left the bar, every cowboy giving him space to leave. Blackjack straightened his purple vest and managed a smile to the crowd of onlookers.

"Now there's a man who just ain't used to losin', folks."

One of the cowboys at the bar, a dusty old man with a red shirt that had seen too many cattle drives, raised his drink.

"That's 'cause Archer Stanton don't ever lose, youngster. Not ever."

Several hours later, a few minutes after eleven at night, Blackjack left the Old Yellow Saloon, and reined his horse, his eyes darting around the street, peering into every shadow created by the full moon. He knew that Marshal Elijah was a days ride out, so if Archer were going to do something, now would be the time. Blackjack chuckled to himself as he raised himself onto his horse. It never fails, a cowboy thinks he's been cheated, and true or not, decides to solve it by drawing his gun, and Blackjack ends it the same way every time, and that cowboy's boss takes offense and decides to take revenge. Normally, it would be to fleece him at the tables, or to beat him up, but Archer was different, he could feel it in his bones. He would want his pound of flesh for his man.

Blackjack started riding out of town, and to his own surprise found himself riding toward Jack Tarver's place. After all, Jack did owe him for saving his life during that bank robbery a few months ago. Perhaps he could see if Jack could talk with Ellie and have her father call off the dogs. It was a long shot, but if anyone could pull it off, it would be that heart of gold Tarver, a trait Blackjack both despised and admired. Blackjack turned his horse on the dusty road to Tarver's place, not noticing the two men following behind him, keeping to the shadows...

Elijah rode back into town, and all was quiet, and for some reason, this didn't settle well with the Marshal. He had decided to return early, as the Miller-Benson dispute had been resolved peacefully. He had been relieved to come back to the familiar town earlier than he had expected. Elijah soon found himself dismounting his horse at the Old Yellow Saloon. He noticed it was quieter than normal, and a quick look around told him the gambler was nowhere in sight. Elijah walked up to the bar and motioned for Harvey to come over.

"So how's business been, Harvey?"

"Fine, Marshal, just fine. "

"Good, good. Have you seen Blackjack tonight?"

"Yeah, he was here for a good while as always, but he left after speaking with Archer Stanton."

"That a fact?"

"Yes sir."

Elijah clicked his teeth as he shook his head. Surely Archie would have better sense than to take revenge for his dead ranch hand. Elijah left the saloon and paced for a moment, unsure where to go, but his legs carried him to the hotel, where he found that Blackjack hadn't come back to yet. Elijah then mounted his horse and rode for the Stanton ranch. Elijah had kept peace in Liberty for over fifteen years, and he sure as hell wasn't going to let an egomaniacal rancher and some two-bit gambler change things...

Carlos and Ben weren't sure exactly when they lost sight of the gambler. They had followed him out of town just like Stanton told them to, and Jake was to meet them on the road. They met Jake, but the point was to have the gambler run right into him, or more to the point, run into a bullet from his gun. The road took them up a hill, and damn if after they cleared the top the gambler was nowhere to be seen. They looked around, and the only horse to be heard was Jake's as he rounded a bunch of trees and rode up to them, looking quizzically at them, they both shrugged their shoulders. Jake smirked as he looked around.

"I can't believe you lost him! Well, he's gotta be around here somewhere. Spread out, check around the homesteads nearby. We find him or else Stanton'll throw a fit."

The men nodded in agreement and began to ride to and fro, and started making their slow way toward the homesteads. Stanton was paying good money to bring the head of that gambler to them, and double if they made it a slow death, and they aimed to collect that extra money...

Blackjack had slowly placed his horse down in some bushes, and lay across him, and waited for his followers to pass. He saw the two men come over the hill, and confirmed they were the same men who were with Stanton earlier. Blackjack knew he was a dead man the longer he stayed in a location by himself in the open, and he quickly looked around and saw a farm just up the road, and could see the light and smoke coming from it. He reached over, and with the butt of his gun hit the horse' shoe until it came partly off. He saw the two men further up the road as another was riding toward them. Blackjack cursed to himself and took the reins of his horse, and staying under heavy brush and trees made his way toward the farmhouse, and hoped his luck would hold on a little longer...

"Come on, Helen, dinner's almost on."

Patricia placed Helen's plate of food on the table, mashed potatoes, corn and some roasted rabbit she had caught earlier in the day. It was hard without Clancy, but they were getting by. At least the farmhouse was paid for thanks to the money from the good-hearted Mr. Daley, and Jack Tarver his son came by every few days and fixed things around the home, which Patricia was grateful for. What she couldn't figure was what would possess Helen to go to that horrible Harvey's Hill. Mr. Tarver had delivered Helen home with her little girl a mess of cobwebs, a torn dress and mud. Helen always was one to play with the boys rather than the girls, and that meant patching up more dresses than any mother should have to. Helen appeared, the fire from the fireplace illuminating her red hair. Helen seemed much happier and talkative after she got home, which made the house feel warm in a way it hadn't since Clancy passed. Helen began to sit down, just as there was a sharp knock at the door. Patricia wasn't expecting any company. Perhaps it was Jack? Patricia opened the door, and concealed something between a frown and outright disgust, if such a thing were possible. The man at the door tipped his gray hat.

"Pardon me, ma'am, my horse's shoe had begun to come off, and I was wondering if I could repair it in your barn before heading on. My name is..."

"Blackjack. Yes, I've heard of you. I suppose it's all right, but don't take too long. We don't care much for gamblers in our home."

"Understood ma'am, understood. My, that food does smell good. I do apologize for interruptin' during your meal time."

"W-would you like to eat with us? We don't have guests that often." Patricia couldn't believe what she was saying. This was the same gambler that took the last of Clancy's money, and besides she had heard stories about him. At the same time, Patricia couldn't bring herself to do the sensible thing and turn him away. Blackjack took a quick look behind him and took his hat off and smiled at Patricia.

"Why, that would be just fine, Mrs..."

"Miller. Mrs. Miller. I believe you've met my husband Clancy."

Blackjack nodded, keeping his smile, trying not to hide the cold chill that ran down his spine. Of all the homes, he found the home of the man who may not have died in that bank job if Blackjack hadn't cleaned him out of the last of his money. Blackjack stepped into the home, and shut the door behind him, and knew that maybe his luck has finally run out...

Chapter 10: Gambler's Call

In which Stanton's men find Blackjack at the Miller homestead, and learn just how tricky the gambler can be...

Helen stared at the gambler sitting across from her with a mixture of fascination and a bit of fear. She had heard her father talk to her about gamblers, men who roamed from town to town, looking for fortune at the card tables, taking good money away from those who worked so hard for it. Blackjack had regaled her with a few stories of some big wins he had in some of the towns he had gone to. She noticed he kept looking toward the windows and door nervously, as if waiting for something. Blackjack looked from the window back to Helen and smiled.

"That was some good food, wouldn't you say, Miss Helen?"

"Always is. You might be able to get more if you quit gambling and settled down."

Patricia smiled as Blackjack shrugged his shoulders.

"I suppose you're right, and someday I might. Right now I just enjoy life, playing cards, traveling around the country..."

"Taking money from hard working men like my Clancy."

Blackjack looked at Patricia for a moment. He was waiting for her to say something like that.

"Ma'am, no one forced your husband to play, and I won fair and square. In truth, he shouldn't have played at all, but when one is

66

desperate to provide for your family, one does whatever one can. That's what eventually got him..."

Blackjack stopped as he noticed the downcast expressions of both Mother and Daughter. He nodded his head. He had said too much, as he usually did. He sighed as he wiped his mouth with his napkin.

"Look, I had an opinion about Clancy. What he did was foolish, and he paid for it, but in the end he saved the Tarver boy, and that counts for a lot in anyone's ledger. Your husband did right by the town. That's what people will remember about him."

Helen looked up and managed a grin. Blackjack smiled back, and stood up, taking the plates from the table

"Thank you for the wonderful meal, Mrs. Miller. Let me get those, and afterward I'll get to taking care of my horse and being on my way."

"Your quite welcome, Mr. Gentry. You don't mind, if we call you that, do you?"

"No ma'am, not a bit. Nice to hear it from such a kind voice."

Patricia looked at Helen and smiled. Blackjack wasn't what she thought he would be. She had pictured him as something like a snake, and she still wouldn't trust him, but she would give him the hospitality of the Miller home. Blackjack then raised himself from his seat and rolled up his sleeves, and walked outside, and took his horse, who stood uncomfortably in the front, and walked him around the house and toward the barn. As he walked, his ears were alive with the sounds of the crickets chirping away, the rustle of the leaves as the soft wind blew, and the click of his horses' damaged hooves on the hard earth. He kept his gaze straight ahead as he moved silently toward the old barn, which looked as if it had just received a new coat of red paint not two days ago. Blackjack stopped for a moment, and smiled. He then began walking until he arrived at the entrance to the barn, where he lit two lamps, placing them on opposite sides of the barn and walked his horse to the center quickly. He then looked around until he found a horseshoe, nails, and a hammer, and set them down on a small round rickety table next to the horse. At no point did his eyes leave the entrance. He figured he was about to have company...

"Come in, my dear Marshal, come in. What brings us the pleasure? Should I call Ellie down?"

Elijah tipped his hat to Archer, but didn't take it off. He stepped inside the house, looking around, and not finding what he'd hope he would. He looked at Archer, and the self-satisfied smile told him everything he needed to know.

"Archer, I heard you crossed paths with that gambler tonight."

"Did you, Elijah? I suppose I did. I had to make sure he knew what it meant to cross me."

"Uh-huh, and how did you in fact mean to do that? I noticed riding in I didn't see your ranch hands here."

Archer, dressed in his blue smoking jacket, sat back down in front of his roaring fireplace. He offered Elijah a cigar and Elijah promptly turned it down with a wave of his hand.

"Esteban had friends here too, Marshall. I can't control what they do on their spare time."

Elijah shook his head as he moved toward the door. As he opened it, he turned to look at Archer, who merely stared at the fire before him.

"For your sake, Archer, they had better not go after the gambler. If they do I'll hold you responsible for whatever happens. I'll not have this kind of behavior in my town!"

Elijah left the ranch and decided to take the main road toward the Tarver ranch. Maybe Blackjack went to the Tarver spread...

Helen had just finished putting up the dishes when she went to her room and took out the horse carving that Chris had made for her when she was sick. She always marveled at the detail that Chris had put into it, and it reminded her of the kindness he and his father had shown her family. She smiled warmly, and was just putting it away when she heard a rustle coming from just outside of her window. She peered out, and saw the silhouette of a lanky man walking silently toward the barn. She could see the silhouetted gun the man was holding in his hand. She ducked the moment she saw the gun, and she almost ran out of her room, but noticed her mother was asleep in her favorite chair. She wondered if that man was going to kill the gambler! Someone had to warn him. Helen tiptoed toward the door, and slowly opened it, and sneaked out, taking care to quietly close the door behind her. She stepped carefully around the corner, just in time to see another man sneaking over their fence from the McClaren place next door onto their farmland, and the man began to make his way toward the shed. She didn't see the first man any longer.

Did he go in and kill the gambler? Or did the gambler get him? She didn't hear a shot. Keeping her head, she made her way toward the barn, being sure to keep her distance from the man just ahead of her.

Blackjack had heard Carlos coming a full minute before he arrived. Blackjack wasn't sure how he knew, but he did. He decided he would avoid waking up Mrs. Miller or her daughter if he could help it. He reached for the horseshoe and readied himself, and after quickly taking a look around, smiled to himself...

Carlos walked carefully through the wheat field. This was the last house in the immediate area, and he had confirmed everything when he saw the gambler escorting his horse to that barn. He had already given a bird whistle to the others, and knew they weren't far behind him. He looked at his gun as he approached the barn, and then thought better of it, and placed his gun silently back in the holster and drew a wicked knife which briefly reflected the moonlight, and he continued his silent trek toward the barn. No sense in killing the gambler only to be gunned down by some farmer thinking they were horse thieves. As he reached the doorway, he stepped to the side, and suddenly the light went out. Carlos lowered himself, and the other men froze where they stood. Helen did the same, only few feet away from Jake, who kept his gun out. Carlos peered into the darkness of the barn, and could hear the breathing of a horse. He heard rustling coming from inside, and took a step inside, and peered further into the darkness. Suddenly he felt something tighten around his feet, and before he could look down and see the noose that tightened around his feet, he found his legs pulled out from underneath him, and he hit the ground with a deadening thud, and found himself hoisted up into the rafters of the barn. He cried for help, and Ben foolishly ran toward the barn, and Blackjack almost laughed as he threw the horseshoe at Ben, striking him dead in the face, knocking him out before he even hit the ground just in front of the barn doors. As he fell, he fired off a shot of his gun, which made Helen jump, as well as Jake, who started moving backward quickly. Farmers from all over would be on them soon if he didn't get away. Helen saw Jake moving backward toward her, and she turned to run, but he did as well, and Helen screamed in surprise as he tripped over her, and the two went end over end into the soft brush. Jake shook his head as he noticed that he had dropped his gun, and scrambled onto his knees and shoving Helen aside started feeling around in the darkness for his gun. He could hear the footsteps of the gambler as he reached for his knife and heard the familiar click of the hammer being drawn back on Blackjack's pearl handled gun. He looked up, and saw death in the eyes of the gambler. Helen moved away from Jake, who began to whimper. He didn't want to go like this, but knew he had it coming. Blackjack raised his gun and pointed it at Jake's head, and smiled to himself as he prepared to send another one of Stanton's men to the abyss, when Helen's voice broke through the darkness.

"He doesn't have a gun."

"Don't matter, little lady. He and his friends were going to kill me."

"So let the marshal have him."

"I'll let the marshal have the other two. *This* one is mine. Now you go on back to the house."

"Before tonight, I thought you were a monster, like everyone else in town, but I learned you aren't. But if you do this, you'll prove everyone right. Is that what you want?"

"You don't understand this, little lady. Maybe when you're grown you will."

"I know right from wrong. My daddy taught me that. But he forgot it himself. For me."

Blackjack looked at Helen for the first time with new eyes, and he saw the strength in those brown eyes that pierced the darkness. Despite everything she's already lost, she still stood for what she knew was right. He took a deep breath, and released the hammer carefully back into the gun. He looked to Jake, who was still shivering.

"Stand up, man. I ain't gonna kill you because this little lady says so, and she just might be right."

Helen smiled at Blackjack as she heard her mother yell her name, and the three of them turned around to see Patricia, followed by Marshal Bronson, running toward them. Patricia grabbed her daughter and held her tight as Elijah stepped forward and surveyed the scene. He grabbed Jake and tied his hands together.

"Busy night, Blackjack?"

"You could say that. What brings you here, Marshal?"

"Heard Stanton had threatened you back in town and thought I'd look for you. Believe it or not I protect the people of this town. Even you."

"I'm flattered, but as you can see I took care of matters myself."

"So I see. I thought with your reputation you would have shot them all dead. You were within rights."

"Maybe," Blackjack said, and looked at Helen and smiled that million-dollar smile, "but I'm not a monster. I'm just a gambler."

Helen smiled back.

Moments later Elijah commandeered a wagon and loaded the men up to ride back to town. He chuckled to himself. He would make

Stanton pay a hefty fine to get these men out of jail. The jail could always use a new coat of paint. He watched Blackjack tip his hat as he said his goodbyes to Patricia and Helen, and mounted his horse and began to ride beside Marshal Bronson. Elijah took a moment before he spoke.

"Nothing has changed here, gambler."

"What do you mean?"

"You may have fooled Patricia and Helen, but you can't fool me. Yes, you spared young Jake here, but you knew you were being chased and brought your fight to the Millers' doorstep. They could've been killed for something you did. You might as well have used them as human shields."

"I would do no such things to the ladies, Marshal. They were never in any danger I couldn't have protected them from."

"But you'd still place them in that danger regardless, eh? Next time, use a rock to find your cover. Leave the Millers alone, or I'll ride you out of town on a blind mule."

Blackjack was about to retort, and then grew silent. Surely he had the skills to protect them, and did, didn't he? But what if he hadn't? Blackjack dropped a little behind the wagon and continued his trek toward town in silence, as he fell deep into his own thoughts, and the only thing to be heard were the squeaky wheels of the wagon as it made its slow way toward Liberty...

Chapter 11: Of Dark Men and Darker Deeds

In which Jack comes face to face with old enemies, and tragedy strikes the Miller home.

Jack wiped his brow as he waved at Miles from across the street as he finished loading the new feed for the horses. Chris was already out of school, and had gone to help Helen do the chores at the Miller home, and Ellie was going to come over for dinner, which made for a perfect evening, in Jack's opinion.

Jack was done with his errands for the day and decided to treat himself to a drink.

Jack walked into the Old Yellow Saloon and made his way to the bar. Harvey came over immediately, a smile crossing his face. He made a passing rub at hair that was no longer on the top of his head and shook Jack's hand. Blackjack was also sitting at the bar, taking a break from the game table.

"How are you, Jack! How's that boy of yours?"

"Fine, just fine, Blackjack. How are things here? You shoot anyone over cards lately?"

"No, no, it's been quiet for me and Harvey here! So what will it be? Surely the man who protected my money from those bandits would let me honor him with a drink! So what's your fancy?"

A familiar voice shot out from a table just behind Jack.

"Whiskey in a clean glass! Jack was always one for the whiskey…"

Jack turned around at the voice and found his hand immediately on the butt of his gun. Jeremy sat at the table, a half cigar hanging from a grinning mouth, and Jeremy looked amused at Jack's surprised look, but there was murder in his eyes as well, but as Jack tried to remember, when was there a time when there wasn't?

"Put that drink on my tab, barkeep! Me and Jack here are old friends, from the War!"

"I can pay for my own drinks, Davis. That goes for both of you."

Jeremy smiled even more at this. Jack hadn't changed a bit, but then his kind never does. Blackjack thought this would be an excellent time to study the contents of his drink, and listened intently.

"So when did they let you out of prison?"

"Not long ago."

"Evidently not long enough. What do you want here, Davis?"

Jeremy smiled that smile that Jack remembered. Usually it came right before he killed someone.

"I came to see you, Jack. I even stopped by your old homestead. My apologies about the missus. I'm sure she was a beautiful woman. Come and sit down a spell, Jack! We got so much to talk about."

Jack moved closer to Jeremy, taking his hand off the butt of his gun. Whatever Jeremy Davis had planned, he wouldn't kill Jack here.

"We don't have anything to talk about. You left me to burn, and you went to prison for it. We have nothing left to say, do we?"

"That's not exactly true, Jack. There is one thing we have left. The gold." Jeremy said, looking closely at Jack for any change of attitude. Jack didn't answer, so Jeremy kept going.

"Color me surprised when we went to that location on the map and found that cave in the mountain empty. I was also surprised to learn you never gave that map to our Captain. You know, takes a lot of money to start over in a new town, with your boy and all. Heard you bought a good size spread not too far out. Now I wonder where you got the money for that?

Jack's eyes narrowed as looked Jeremy dead in his eyes.

"None of your business, Davis, but there was nothing in that mountain. You came out here for nothing I can or would give you."

The smile left Jeremy's face, and his anger cracked through the veneer of coolness.

"No man leaves something like that behind, Tarver. No man. I want that gold, or so help me I'll make you give it up. I got some men with me, heck even Godfrey came. Surely you remember him. He ain't forgot you."

Jeremy downed the last of his tequila and stood up. He looked around a moment, and saw that the Marshal was approaching.

"I would keep my boy close to me if I were you, Tarver. Either that, or you give me my gold by tomorrow. We meet at the hotel just down the street tomorrow at noon."

Jack stood up quickly and grabbed Jeremy by his collar. There was no way he was about to let Chris be threatened by this monster. Blackjack's hand reflexively went to his gun handle.

"If you come anywhere near my boy, Davis..."

Jeremy broke Jack's hold. Whatever else had happened, prison had strengthened Jeremy.

Jeremy tipped his hat at Jack, and lowered his voice.

"Then you'll get me my gold. Don't go thinkin' about tellin' anyone around here about it. Some of these townsfolk might kill you for it. Hell, even the gambler here might, and you KNOW he heard everything. God's sakes, it's gettin' so you just can't trust folks no more!"

Jeremy walked out of the saloon, tipping his hat as he passed Marshal Bronson, who walked in, giving Jeremy a sideways glance. Harvey started to get Elijah's favorite bourbon, first putting down the shotgun that he was holding in case something happened. Elijah didn't take long to notice something was wrong. Even Blackjack looked agitated.

"Hello, Jack. Something wrong? You look like you just saw a ghost!"

"Elijah, I think I'm going to need some help…"

Jack sat down with Elijah and started telling him the entire story, starting with Virginia Hill. Surprisingly enough, he let Blackjack listen in as well…

Jeremy climbed up on his saddle and rode out of town, and before long met Jensen, one of his men, who had been waiting for him. Jensen was chewing a stick of wheat, and pulled it out long enough to ask the obvious.

"I take it he don't have the gold?"

"Oh, he's got the gold all right. I gave him until tomorrow noon to come up with it, or we take his boy."

Jensen smiled.

"He ain't givin' it up."

"Yeah, I know. That's why I sent Godfrey to grab his boy an hour ago."

Ellie looked in her closet. So many dresses to choose from. Which one would woo Jack tonight? She shook her head as she reviewed her options. Not only must she please him, but she has to get the approval of his son as well! Ellie hated doing this, but it was all she could to protect her family ranch. She liked Jack, but didn't really feel anything past that. Her father's health was failing, and she had to do everything she could to make his remaining days happy ones, even at the expense of Jack. She found a nice blue dress that she hadn't worn in a very long time, not since her last suitor left. Ellie put the dress on and looked at herself in the mirror. She didn't hear her father enter the room.

"You look like gold, Ellie, pure gold. Just like your mother."

"Thanks, daddy. I'm about to go meet Jack. Wish me luck!"

Stanton looked at his daughter and smiled. He wanted her to be happy, and to be with the man she wants. She was about to give that up for him, but now...

"Ellie, dear, before you leave, there's something about Jack Tarver that you should know..."

Chris put the last nail in the once broken fence just as one of the pigs came dangerously close to licking his face. Chris jumped up and fell on the ground, and heard the familiar laughter of Helen behind him. He stood up and brushed the dirt off of him, glaring at the pig the entire time. Helen kept laughing as she walked over and put an assuring hand on his shoulder. Her hand also had some dirt on it, as she had just been feeding the livestock, and she was wearing jeans and an old red button down shirt. Chris was surprised, as always, at how beautiful she looked, even when dressed tomboyish. Chris kicked some dirt toward the pig, and then found himself laughing as well. He was still being punished by his father for coming home so late last night, but he was allowed to come over to help the Millers take care of the farm. He was at least glad for that. He looked at Helen as soon as his laughter subsided.

"I guess the pig won that round! I was meanin' to ask you, who do you think those men were last night?"

Helen shook her head, her face looking more serious.

"I don't know, but I don't think they were up to anything good. Did you tell your father about them?"

"Naw, not yet. I'll tell him tonight."

Helen kicked some dirt awkwardly at her feet. She looked worried.

"Make sure you do. I don't have a good feeling about them..."

Chris didn't answer, his gaze being drawn toward the house, where he noticed several riders approaching. He motioned for Helen to look toward the house, and she did so, wondering who those men were, but they weren't close enough to the house to get a good look. Chris and Helen started to make their way toward the house.

Patricia was just finishing cleaning the house and was about to start dinner soon, and hoped that Jack would let Chris stay over. She thanked God for the Tarvers and their kindness, and she couldn't help but smile as she looked at Chris and Helen outside. Patricia was glad he was here, and what he's done for Helen. She wondered if she and Clancy had ever been so adventurous. She retreated into her memories of Clancy, as she did so often these days. She started to cut the potatoes when she heard horses approached from the front. She curiously walked to the door and opened it, and saw five men she wasn't familiar with, but remembered the man in front. The one who was the brother of Jack's deceased wife. She waved at them as she emerged from the door. Godfrey dismounted, followed by the other men, and came toward her. He was looking around the entire time.

"Mrs. Miller, is it? I came to get Chris. Could you bring him here? His father wants him home."

"Of course, of course. He's out back with my daughter. Let me call him! Chris!"

Chris and Helen had already been walking back to the house when Chris heard his name.

He began to move a little faster when he heard Patricia call out again, and this time he was close enough to see the men and Patricia. He looked at the men, none of whom reputable, and Helen suddenly grabbed his hand, and whispered into his ear.

"Chris! That man! The third one from the front. Look at his hand!"

Chris looked at his hand, and found that it was bandaged. Like the hand he hit last night to free Helen! Chris and Helen stopped dead in their tracks. Patricia looked over and called for them to come closer.

"Chris, your uncle has come to take you home!"

Chris looked at Godfrey. That was no uncle of his! His grip tightened in Helen's hand as he started to move back. Godfrey turned and saw Chris and Helen, and started moving toward them, and two of the men with him started to follow.

"That ain't no uncle of mine, Mrs. Miller! Helen, RUN!"

Chris and Helen started running toward the barn, and Godfrey and his men started giving chase, pulling their guns out and yelling for them to stop. Patricia panicked as she realized her mistake. One of the men, a large man with a bowler hat and missing eye started to move toward the action when Patricia pushed him into the fence with all of her might. The man, known as Buckner, had been drawing his gun at that moment when he found himself falling into the white fence, his gun discharging as he fell. Helen spun around as she heard the shot, almost lifting Chris off his feet. He had hoped to get to his horse that was saddled on the other side, but knew that may not happen now. Luckily, the other men turned to see what had happened as well. Buckner shook his head as he looked up, and saw Patricia Miller look at him incredulously, and then looked down, and Buckner followed her gaze to the bullet hole that had entered her chest. Patricia staggered as she closed her hand on the wound, feeling the blood leaving her body. She looked toward Helen and tried to call out, but could not. She prayed that Chris would protect Helen always, and Patricia Miller, daughter of Thomas and Sally Hyatt of Georgia, fell to the ground dead. Helen screamed as she saw her mother fall and tried to run toward her, but Chris grabbed her and moved her toward the barn. Helen cried as Chris nearly carried her to the barn, and lifted her onto the horse and could hear the approaching footsteps of Godfrey and his men, and mounted the horse, putting his arms around Helen. They raced from the opposite end of the barn, and Godfrey stopped running and looked to Hansen, who lifted his rifle and took careful aim.

"Make it a good shot. We need them alive. At least, we need the boy alive."

Hansen took careful aim, and fired.

Chapter 12: Sunset

In which the various townspeople of Liberty learn of the danger to the children, and Jack releases a rage not seen since the war...

Jack threw open the door to his home and didn't bother to close it, barely noticing that his home had been ransacked hours before by Godfrey and his men. Jack went into his room, and moved his bed aside and hoped Davis' men weren't very observant. He removed three of the floorboards and brought out a metal box. He reached into his pocket and drew a small rusty key and inserted it into the lock. His hands trembled in quiet rage as he turned the key and opened the box. He couldn't get the image of his son out of his head. He took the belt of bullets from the case and replaced his plain belt. It had been years, even before the war that Jack felt he needed this belt, but things were different now, and the past had a way of sneaking up on one. Jack and Elijah had arrived just in time to find Patricia's body and Chris' dead horse at the Miller place. Jack left Elijah there, fear struck and furious. Jack cursed his own mercy. He should have chased Jeremy and Godfrey down and shot them for their betrayal years ago. No one would have faulted him for it. And now...

Jack checked his gun and reloaded it. He cursed himself so loudly he didn't even hear Elijah walk into the house. Elijah held his rifle by his side, and walked into the bedroom and looked hard at Jack.

"I suppose you're taking off to find your boy?"

"What do you think?"

Jack stood up and started loading his rifle. Elijah leaned by the door.

"We should wait 'till I form a posse."

"Go form it. I'm going to get my boy."

"Really? Where will you go? I don't recall you mentioning their hideout. Davis is probably back in town waiting for you. So either way, you're coming back to town with me."

Jack stopped and looked at Elijah. His face was hard as stone, and Elijah recognized the look. Only the old gunfighters, men who barely exist anymore, had that look right before a whole lot of people died. Jack wanted to throw a comment back at Elijah, but he couldn't because he knew Elijah was right. Jack walked past Elijah and out of the house. He mounted his horse, and Elijah walked out and got in the wagon that held Patricia Miller's body. Someone had to take her back to town. They started their way back, and the trip was a silent one full of anger and frustration on both men's parts. Elijah looked over at Jack as they came with sight of town.

"Jack, I know men like you. You think this whole thing is your problem to solve, but I tell you it's not. No one will blame you. Those men killed our Patricia and took two of our own children. That makes it everyone's problem."

Jack didn't answer as they rode, and made their way to the Marshals' office, and as they stopped in front they found a small crowd of townspeople forming behind them. Miles was there, and looked at the body of Patricia Miller in the wagon, His head fell in despair as he took his gray bowler hat off. Elijah stood up in the wagon as Jack dismounted. Elijah looked at the people solemnly.

"People of Liberty, I need as many able men as possible to form a posse! Some bandits have killed Patricia Miller and taken her daughter, along with Chris Tarver. We're going to find them and bring them back safely. I ain't gonna lie to you, these men are very dangerous. Who's gonna help us?"

The people spoke among themselves for a moment, and Jack shook his head. He knew he and the Marshal would be alone in this. Jack started to enter the office when he heard what he didn't expect.

"Hells bells, Elijah! I'm in!"

"That Tarver boy tutored my son! I'm in, too!"

"Jack saved me and my wife at the bank! You couldn't drag me away from this one!"

Jack turned to face the people of Liberty as men started running for their horses and guns.

Miles came up to Jack and put a hand on his shoulder. The little big man smiled at Jack.

"Don't you worry about a thing, Jack. We'll find the children! We take care of our own here!"

Jack looked at Miles, and then at the rest of the town, once quiet, now awake with anger as men rode to get more help, and mothers took their children home. Elijah went in and handed rifles to anyone who came for one, and before long there were thirty men strong standing outside, and Elijah quickly deputized them. They formed small search parties and took off for the outskirts of town. Many of the old men in town watched with a small glee. They haven't seen this kind of commotion in years. Even banker Jim Daley, still wearing his napkin from dinner ran forward, dressed in his good suit, holding a shotgun in his good arm. Jack was about to jump on a horse and follow when a panting Harvey Smith, who had run all the way down the street from the saloon, stopped him. Harvey tried to speak, and then settled for handing Jack a note. Jack opened the note, read it, and crushed it in anger as Elijah came to see what it was about. Blackjack had followed after Harvey.

"It's a note from Jeremy. He wants me to deliver the gold, alone in two days. Just outside Colorado near the mountains. Damn that man! He just doesn't understand what that place was!"

Harvey shook his head in agreement as he began to get his breath back.

"Yeah, one of his men dropped it off not even an hour ago. I didn't see which way he rode out. Sorry, Jack."

Blackjack had seen which way he went but said nothing. No point in saying what wasn't truly important. That rider wasn't going the right way deliberately.

Jack gave Harvey a pat on his shoulder and turned to go back to Elijah when Mr. Peacock, a tall lanky man with a long nose and long arms and legs ran forward, trailed by his sons, Manny and Alex, who were doing their best to keep up with their fathers' long strides.

"Jack, we heard what happened to Helen and Chris! Manny and Alex have something I think you ought to hear! Go on, boys, tells Mr. Tarver what you told me!" said Mr. Peacock, motioning his boys to step forward. Elijah walked over as they began to speak.

Everyone listened intently as the boys recounted everything that happened at Harvey's Hill. After they were done Mr. Peacock patted his sons on the shoulder and led them away. Jack ran to his horse and jumped on, and rode toward Harvey's Hill as fast as his horse would take him, followed by Sheriff Elijah, Miles, and Jim Daley. No one had noticed that Blackjack had already mounted his horse and rode out in the opposite direction out of town...

Archer Stanton paced back and forth on the expensive red rug he had gotten from somewhere in Asia. It had been several hours, and he was curious as to how her dinner went with Tarver when one of his ranch hands, Enrique, burst through the door.

"Jefe! I just got back from town! The place is *muy* loco! The son of Senior Tarver and one of his friends has been taken by bandits!"

Archer nearly dropped his cigar.

"Wait-wasn't Ellie at Tarvers'?

"I don't know, but Tarver and the Marshal have formed posse and have started looking for the boy and his friend!"

Archer grabbed Enrique and moved him quickly back to the door.

"Go and get Rico, load up and get my horse ready! We need to find those men first!"

Enrique left to find Rico while Stanton grabbed his derringer and shotgun. No doubt the kidnappers were the same men who wanted the gold from Tarver. Stanton had wanted Ellie to get more information about that from Jack, after Rico had heard the conversation between Jack and Jeremy Davis in the bar yesterday. If he could somehow get the location of the gold first...perhaps an allegiance was in order? No doubt his men believed he was concerned for the boy and his friend, but honestly Archer could care less. His ranch-that his family had for forty years-was going to be lost unless he took drastic measures. Maybe he could save the boy in the end, but if not...

Moments later Archer and his ranch hands rode out. Archer had a pretty good idea where the bandits would be hiding. They were never aware they were being followed...

Ellie had just ridden up the small hill toward the Miller home when she heard the first shot. She stopped her horse, and after a moment kept riding, but just off of the main road. She reached into her saddlebag and found the small silver gun there, but left it for the time being. She rode until she saw the Miller home. She was still quite far away, but close enough to see a group of men running after two people, and she dismounted her horse and hid in some bushes and watched. She saw the two people being chased shot off of their horse, and went down so violently even from afar Ellie winced. She looked closer and recognized one of them as Chris! Her mouth fell open in surprise as she saw Chris and the other, who must be Helen, being picked up by two of the men. Helen seemed to struggle, but Chris wasn't moving. The men tied them both up and put them on a horse and rode toward the Tarver home, far off the main road. Ellie shook her head and remounted her horse and rode to the Miller home. When she arrived, she didn't bother to dismount. She looked down at the body of Patricia. Ellie shook her head. These men must be the ones her father had told her about, the ones who wanted the gold Jack had. Ellie turned her horse and rode down the road toward the Tarver home. When she arrived she entered the home only to find no sign of Jack, and the house had already been ransacked. It seemed that no piece of furniture was left upright, and so the men must not have found the gold. They must have bypassed the house, but there were no other homes east of them except...the abandoned house at Harvey's Hill! Ellie remounted her horse and rode toward the abandoned home. She would make sure the children were at the house and then let Jack know. That gold wasn't worth the lives of those children. Of course her father would agree with that. She was doing the right thing. It had been a long time since that had happened.

Chapter 13: The Meek and the Mighty

Chris and Helen find themselves at the mercy of Jeremy Davis and his gang, and Helen finds something she did not know she had...

Helen had been silent as they rode toward Harvey's Hill. She kept thinking about her mother. These men took her away, the last of her family was now gone. She didn't cry, almost willing it not to happen. She was determined to not give them the satisfaction of seeing her pain. She turned to see if Chris was all right. He was still draped over the saddle of the horse next to her. She wanted to lean over and nudge him but didn't dare. She couldn't tell if he was breathing or not. The way he went down after the horse was shot...the only reason she was all right was because she fell on him, cushioning her fall. She silently prayed that he was still alive, that she wasn't truly alone, surrounded by these evil men. Soon they arrived at Harvey's Hill, and upon stopping the very man who just killed her mother roughly pulled her off of the horse. Helen spat in his face and was slapped across the face hard for her trouble. The man who was waiting for them laughed as they were walked past him into the home, where she was sat down on the floor. Chris was unceremoniously dumped in a heap next to her. She quickly checked to see if he was alive. She let out a sigh of relief as she discovered he was still breathing, but had a nasty gash on the side of his head that was dried with blood. She tore part of her pant leg and looked to one of the men, a disheveled looking man named Riley, who had just entered the room.

"He needs water."

"So what do I care?" spat Riley back at her, and sat down at the rotted dining table and started shuffling playing cards.

"He'll catch a fever and die if I can't clean this wound."

Riley shuffled the cards for a moment, and then thought better of it and grabbed a saddlebag and removed the canteen and threw it at Helen's feet, and sat back down and started shuffling cards again. Helen tore off a piece of her pant leg and began using it and the water to clean Chris' head. She wiped off the blood and cleaned it as best she could, and then with another torn pant leg she bandaged his head. She had just finished when the door opened and several men walked in. One of them, the one who had been waiting for them, walked toward her. He was a large man, with a great unkempt dark beard and long black hair. He wore a jacket that looked like an old Union soldier's uniform. He bent over slightly and looked her over, and then Chris, and then his gaze returned to her.

"Don't worry, girl. This boy's father pony up with our gold and you're both free to go."

Helen's eyes narrowed as she glared at him.

"You people killed my mother. I pray that Jack Tarver puts a bullet in all of you!"

Jeremy shook his head in agreement as he raised himself up.

"I'd be mad if I were you, too. Your mother was an accident, but it happened. You need to deal with your own life now. The boy gonna live or not?"

Helen nodded her head. She knew there were no other words to say. She had entertained the idea of escaping, but with Chris injured, she couldn't leave him. These men would kill them anyway, gold or not. She was sure of that now. Helen looked hard at every man who walked into that room, and them turned to check on Chris, who was slowly starting to move his fingers. She said a small prayer and held Chris' hand. For now it was all she could do.

"So what's the plan now, Jeremy? We got the kid but the gold wasn't at Tarver's home."

Jeremy took a drink of whiskey from his flask and looked over at Helen and Chris. He shrugged his shoulder and looked back at Riley and Godfrey.

"The plan is, because you fools killed the Miller woman the whole damn town is looking for us, and we'll never escape the county to Colorado. We need a new place to hole up while we deal with Jack. Either way, a fight's coming, and we better be ready."

Jeremy looked back at Riley and motioned him to go upstairs.

"Get to the roof, Riley. You should have a good view of the entire area for nearly a mile. Git going and holler if you see anyone."

Riley grabbed his cards and ran up the stairs. Jeremy then turned to Godfrey and spoke just out of earshot of the others.

"If we're lucky Tarver may take a few of us out before we get the gold. Less men to split it with is a good thing."

Godfrey smiled, and went back outside, while Jeremy and the two remaining men looked to Helen.

"So here you are, girl. Want we should cut you in on that gold? Heard around these parts that your Pa got shot for trying to steal from the bank. Man after my own heart."

Helen grabbed a piece of wood and threw it at Jeremy, but missed, as Jeremy never bothered to move, but smiled.

"You piece of trash!" Helen yelled," My father was a good man who tried to save me. He's nothing like you!"

"That so? So he did it to save you, and that makes him better? No, little lady, you got it all wrong. We all got reasons. Tarver had his, too. I mean, he had the gold to help you out, and didn't. So what does that make him?"

"Maybe there isn't any gold."

Jeremy nodded his head at that notion. He had thought that Tarver might have spent it all or lost it gambling, but that didn't change the fact that he put himself and Godfrey in prison for ten years.

"Could be that's the case. Don't matter. Tarver's got a lot to answer for."

"So do you."

"We all do one way or the other, don't we girl?"

Helen was about to give Jeremy a retort when Chris groaned in pain. She turned and gripped his hand tightly. Chris slowly opened his eyes and tried to look around, but Helen made sure he stayed down. Chris looked at her questioningly.

"Where are we?"

"We're back at Harvey's Hill, Chris. They have us, and they want the gold your father has."

Chris tried once again to raise himself, but a sharp pain shot through his head prompting him to set his head back down.

"We don't have any gold."

Helen looked back at Jeremy, who was talking to one of the other men.

"I'm not so sure they care, Chris."

Ellie looked through the bushes at the house. She had gotten quite close on her own after she came through the creek bed, and was trying to avoid the man who had just climbed onto the rooftop. She tried to get a count of the number of men, and then head back to town to let everyone know. She checked her gun to make sure it was loaded. It was a small gun, but had saved her on a few occasions. Ellie remembered playing with the Harvey girl before she was killed here. She remembered that day, and wondered if-after this is over- it wouldn't be best to just destroy what was left of the house. Too many evil memories here. She looked around herself to make sure they didn't have a man patrolling the area, and then moved as quietly as possible to get a better vantage point of the front door. Ellie decided to move even closer to the house, as there was a bunch of bushes under the window of the living room. She moved right up to the window and quickly peered in. She saw several men sitting at a table, and she could just barely make out Helen, and what must be Chris. They were sitting on the same side as the window, so they were hard to make out. Ellie listened in as Jeremy had his conversation with Helen. Ellie nodded her head in admiration. Strong girl. Lost her mother and captured, but lost none of her fire. Ellie heard a commotion coming from the roof as Riley went inside and she hid lower in the bushes. She overheard Riley as he ran halfway down the stairs.

"We got three riders headed this way, Jeremy!"

All of the men got up, some going outside, some upstairs. Jeremy told Riley to head back to the roof and wait there, and Jeremy, with the help of one of the other men, took Helen and Chris to the far side of the living room, right by the kitchen door. Ellie looked back through the window and noticed this, and proceeded to crawl toward the back of the house. She knew there was a kitchen door out back. Maybe she could get the kids out during whatever distraction the riders would give her? It was worth a try. Ellie noted that one of the men mounted a horse and rode in the direction of the oncoming party. She stood up the moment she rounded the back of the house and raised her gun as she approached the kitchen door. She slowly wrapped her hand around the door handle and moved it slowly. The door creaked slightly, which made her stop and wince, and she tried it again, and was able to open the door without further sound. She walked slowly into the house, making sure the door shut silently behind her. Ellie walked slowly to the door that led to the living room, and knelt down. She heard the hooves of multiple horses arriving, and readied herself to grab the kids. She waited, expecting to hear gunfire, but nothing except the door opening, and Jeremy speaking.

"So what do we have here? What do you want?"

"I want in on that gold. The posse will be here soon, and you know you can't keep them here, but I know where you can until Tarver comes up with the gold. I just want my cut. Can we deal?"

"Suppose we can. I would like to know who I'm dealin' with, though."

Ellie almost fainted as she heard the voice. How could this be?

"Stanton. Archer Stanton."

Chapter 14: Saints and Sinners

In which everyone in Liberty takes the road given them, and the choices they've made come to a head.

Jeremy fingered the holster on his gun, all the while admiring the small but stout old man in front of him. It takes some kind of guts to just walk in and introduce himself like that. Luckily for Archer, Jeremy respected guts. Unfortunately for Archer, the others didn't. Jeremy heard the hammer cocking on several guns. He waved his men off and stepped forward.

"Settle down, boys, just give the man a moment. All right, old-timer, as you can see we're an impatient bunch, so let's get to it. What's your plan?"

Archer cleared the lump in his throat, wiping the sweat from his brow with his embroidered handkerchief. His voice almost cracked as he spoke, but he was a leader of men, and steeled himself, and thought of Ellie.

"I get twenty percent of whatever Tarver gives you. In return you all come to my ranch, where no one will think to look, and Tarver will have no choice but to pay up. If you stay here, the posse will be along soon, and you won't stand a chance, not after killing the Miller woman."

Archer finished and looked hard at Jeremy, who looked to Godfrey, who leaned against a wall. Godfrey nodded his head. Jeremy smiled. They could always kill the old fool once this was over anyway.

"All right, Stanton. Twenty percent it is. Let's get going. You lead us, and so help me if I think you're not straight with us I'll plug you myself!"

Ellie slowly backed away from the door and crawled back outside. She knew they were desperate for money, but to hold children ransom? The mere thought of that turned her stomach, but what to do now? If he's caught with them, he'll go to prison, where he'll surely die, or be shot, either by the posse or one of the kidnappers! She cursed the brashness of her father, a trait she also shared. Unless she could find a way for him to get out of this, it would be the end of him. Ellie backed further into the bushes and started to make her way back to her horse when she found her self grabbed and a hand went over her mouth, silencing her. She violently struggled to break the man's grip; while the man told her to stop struggling or her pretty body would get hurt. Ellie recognized the voice and stopped moving, prompting the man to release her. She turned to face Blackjack.

"What are you doing here?" she whispered.

He looked at her and shook his head disapprovingly.

"Me? Why don't you explain why your Pa decided to lie with snakes?"

Ellie was about to hurl an insult his way, but thought better of it.

"I thought they were more your taste."

"Nah, I prefer the gambling sort. Kidnapping kids? What's the fun in that?"

Ellie almost wanted to smile, but she remembered that he killed her friend, and looked back toward the house.

"They're gonna take those kids back to my father's ranch and hide until Tarver comes up with that gold. In exchange he gets a cut of it."

Blackjack shook his head. He figured as much, but one question nipped at him.

"Your Pa's a high roller in these parts. Why take this kind of risk?"

"He's doing it for me. He owes certain...parties a lot of money. The ranch is almost broke. So why are you here?"

Blackjack made his way back through the brush toward their horses, not answering her, because in truth he wasn't sure himself. He owed Tarver nothing, and in fact Tarver owed him for saving him at the bank during that robbery. He had never really spoken with Chris, and knew of Helen only by reputation of her father and mother. He shrugged his shoulders.

"Always wanted to be a hero."

"You? I doubt that. There must be some money in it somewhere."

"If there is, I haven't seen it. Ain't as if I haven't been lookin', either."

After trudging through the creek bed they made their way to their horses and mounted up.

Ellie looked worriedly at the direction of the house, and could almost hear the commotion as the men prepared to leave. She looked back at Blackjack, who hadn't yet mounted his horse.

"So what now?"

"Now you're going to head back home, and get ready to save those kids, 'cause there's a fight coming to your doorstep, and they need to be out of the way."

Ellie shook her head.

"No! You're gonna bring the posse to my home! My father..."

"You're father chose his path, woman. If he's lucky he'll play as if he were an unwilling party, and hope the posse will buy that. Either way, his life ain't worth those children, and you know it. Now get moving."

Ellie turned her horse and galloped as fast as she could toward her home, confused at Blackjack, just as she thought she had him figured out. Blackjack watched her leave, and then watched as scant minutes later Stanton and the Davis gang rode hard and fast in the same direction, with the children in tow. Blackjack rode around to the front of the house, and dismounted his horse and looked in the opposite direction, where the posse would be coming from. He heard the cocking of the gun behind him, just in the house.

"Good thing I left late or else I woulda' missed you, gambler. How about you throw that hog iron to the ground?"

Blackjack slowly pulled his gun from its holster and dropped it to the ground. He turned around to face Godfrey, who had him dead to rights. Godfrey stepped forward, grinning from ear to ear, a sight to behold from the thinness of his face. Blackjack tried to play it off as best he could.

"You know, I was just looking for you. I was hoping to make a deal, but darn the luck if someone else didn't beat me to it."

"Really? That's bad luck. It's also too bad I've heard of you, Blackjack. Heart o' Gold gambler I hear. Except of course that stuff in Carson City. I'm sure that eats away at you every day, man. It's a shame you ain't gonna get a chance to make up for it!"

Blackjack looked just behind Godfrey as he prepared to shoot.

"You might want to look behind you, friend."

Godfrey scoffed at this.

"Please, don't ruin this with some stupid attempt to save yourself. It's kind of embarrassing. You just played your last bluff!"

Godfrey then heard the voice behind him.

"Not really."

Godfrey turned too late as Jack butted him in the head with his rifle. Godfrey crumpled to the ground in a heap. Blackjack noticed Elijah and Miles coming from around the back of the house. Blackjack looked down at Jack, who was tying up Godfrey.

"Why did you wait so long? I thought you were gonna let him shoot me!"

"I know. I just wanted to make sure we were even."

Blackjack laughed at this. Tarver wasn't as simple as he had originally thought.

Elijah stood in front of them, solemn.

"So what *are* you doing here, Blackjack? Just for the record, this had better be good."

"I assure you, Marshal, it is. It damn sure is…"

Blackjack quickly told his story, of course embellishing some things, and leaving some things out entirely, like Ellie, and her father's reasoning for coming to Harvey's Hill.

"I tell you, Marshal, Stanton was coming with one of his ranch hands looking for the kids when they overran him and grabbed him, too. Looks like they headed for the Stanton spread."

Elijah nearly spat at Blackjack as Jim Daley rode from behind them, with Doc Harrison not far behind holding Jack and Elijah's horses by the reins.

"So what made you come out here first?"

"Civic duty, Marshal, my civic duty." Blackjack said, and knew that it was very nearly the truth.

"You expect us to believe that?" Elijah retorted.

Jack mounted his horse. This was getting worse every moment, and worse still that he hadn't thought about Ellie since meeting Davis at the saloon earlier that day, and now she and her father were in danger. Jack winced at the thought, and wondered what he would do when this was over. He had, inadvertently or not, brought this on the townspeople of Liberty, and felt all the guiltier for it. He snapped back from his reverie to hear the last thing Elijah had said to Blackjack.

"I believe him, Elijah. We need to get the rest of the posse to the Stanton Ranch. Jim, can you do it?"

Jim Daley tipped his hat with his good arm and smiled.

"I'm already on my way, Jack!"

Blackjack and Miles mounted their own horses while Elijah tied Godfrey's unconscious body to the saddle of his own horse, and mounted up, and before long they were heading toward the Stanton ranch and what they hoped would be the end of the long day…

Jeremy Davis and his gang rode hard and fast toward the Stanton ranch, heeding the directions Stanton was giving them, keeping them off the main roads and avoiding potential confrontations with the local farmers. Helen kept quiet during the trip, unsure what to do, with her hands tied and one of the men holding her. She looked over at Chris, who had now fully regained his senses enough to know that they were in a bad situation. Chris could see the fear in Helen's eyes, even as her pretty face had transformed into a granite expression of anger. Chris found himself looking at Stanton, and shook his head. He couldn't believe Stanton would involve himself with these men. Before long they had arrived at the Stanton ranch, where both Ellie and Consuela were waiting for them. Ellie had told Consuela what was happening, and what was going to happen, and Consuela decided to stay. Ellie and Consuela quickly prepared the house for their arrival. It took some doing, and Ellie prayed she had done the right thing, even though it truly meant the end for the Stanton Ranch. She watched from the top of the hill as the riders approached, and she was relieved that they had arrived safely. Consuela ran into the house, while Ellie waved at them. The riders stopped and dismounted quickly, running the horses around the back, which is just what Ellie had hoped they would do. Davis jumped off of the horse and regarded Ellie for a moment, and motioned for the men to get those kids off the horses. The men entered the house in a whirlwind of action, two men running to take positions upstairs, and two others in the living room keeping watch out of the windows. Jeremy took a quick look around the room, noting the fine furniture and the expensive carpets and paintings all over. He looked outside and took note of the bushes a few yards away from the house, and the big oak tree standing smack in the middle. Not the best place for anyone to take cover, he thought. Davis hadn't kidded himself for a moment. They had a day, maybe two if they were lucky, before half the damn town arrived at his doorstep. He ran out back and also counted the distance to the stables some fifty yards away.

Ellie waited until Helen and Chris were forcibly sat down at the living room sofas. Ellie avoided the groping hands of a large thuggish man and checked first on Chris' head, which still had a nasty gash as she removed the makeshift bandages Helen had made.

"Are you all right, Chris? Let me take a look at this. That looks like that hurt quite a bit. I'll have Consuela bring some bandages for you. Helen, are you all right?"

Helen didn't answer at first, simply glared, not at Ellie, but at Archer standing behind her.

"I'm fine. Just tryin' to figure out why your Pa is doing this."

Archer put a hand on Ellie's shoulder and smiled at Helen.

"I'm just trying to protect my daughter, to make sure she's taken care of. I may lose her if I don't! Even if I get killed because of this!"

Chris shook his head in dismay. He'd heard this before, from a man just as desperate.

"Clancy."

Archer and Ellie looked at Chris, and so did Helen.

"Thinkin' like that's what got Clancy Miller killed. You both love your daughters, and you'll wind up just like Clancy in the end. What would Ellie have without you? What does Helen have now that her father-and mother-are gone?"

The words hit both Helen and Ellie like a slap in the face. Tears welled in Helen's eyes as she looked into Ellie's, and Ellie saw the pain in Helen's face, and noted for the first time how much they looked alike. Archer scoffed at this, but his voice betrayed his worry.

"Nonsense, boy. Clancy's situation is totally different. I'm saving the future for Ellie, as I always have. She'll have the best of everything, my little girl with strawberry hair. We just have to wait a bit longer. Your father's gold..."

"There ain't no gold! There never was!"

"But the map from the war..."

"If there was gold, don't you think I'd know?"

"Don't heed Tarver's boy, Stanton. There's gold with him, I stake my life on it. Hell, I'll stake *yours*," said Davis, walking back into the room. He looked around for a moment and noticed that something was amiss.

"Where's Godfrey? Did any of you yahoos see Godfrey?"

Charlie Parks looked over from one of the windows and shrugged his shoulders.

"He said he had to get a few things and would be right behind us!"

"What'd he need to get?"

"How should I know?"

"You ain't no darn good, you know that Charlie?" Davis said, sitting down in what was Archer's favorite chair near the fireplace. Davis took his gun out and inspected it, looking around. Archer and Ellie sat next to the children, Archer holding Ellie as tightly as he could.

Davis waved his gun around the room as he regarded it.

"Look at this. This is the way we were supposed to live. Toiled through that damn war and for what? Free a bunch of people I could care less about! I wanted to make a name for myself, you know, like Lee and Grant! That didn't happen, no thanks to your Pa."

When Davis said "Pa" he pointed the gun straight at Chris, who braced himself.

Davis kept the gun pointed at Chris even as Stanton tried to talk him down.

"Don't shoot, Davis! You-you need him alive, remember?"

Davis didn't seem to act as if he heard Stanton, suddenly filled with a rage at Jack Tarver, and here was his boy in front of him, surely the most important thing in his life, or was he?

"You father robbed me of everything, boy. I take you and we're even. Or maybe I take the woman. I heard he was sweet on you, Ellie, was it?"

Davis said this as he kept the gun on Chris. Archer placed himself between them.

"No, no, well it may look that way, but Ellie was really trying to get with Tarver to get his money. You know, his money would put us in good standing."

Chris looked at Ellie and Archer and at first didn't want to believe it, but one look on Ellie's face told him that every word was true. His stomach soured as he looked at them both. Davis only managed to shake his head in stark disbelief.

"And they say *I'm* bad. You whoring out your daughter to a Negro so you can make some money? Hell, even I wouldn't do that, and *I'm* wanted for murder in five states! You are some truly sick individuals!"

Davis looked around for a moment and shouted back,

"Where's that Mexican gal at? Somebody have her bring me some whiskey. I know it's here somewhere!"

Chris looked at Davis hard. He remembered the stories he had heard about Davis. A murderer ten times over for all the helpless prisoners he killed during the war. A man without honor, his father had said. Chris held Helen's trembling hand, and felt her steady herself. Chris knew full well a man like Davis wouldn't let them live no matter what his father gave him, and the lives of the Stantons were just as forfeit. Chris promised himself that the first opportunity he got he would get himself and Helen out of there...

Consuela heard her name being yelled from downstairs. She almost jumped when she heard it, and quickly spread the last of the kerosene on top of Ellie's clothes in her closet. Consuela hated to do it to such fine clothing, but Ellie believed it had to be done. Luckily for them, the other men were in adjoining rooms, keeping their concentration on the quickly looming shadows in the fields as night began to fall. Consuela quickly closed the closet door. The next time she came into this room, she would know what she needed to do.

Chapter 15: The Siege of Stanton Ranch

In which Jack and the people of Liberty take on the Davis Gang, and Ellie tries to do the right thing...

"So what now?"

Jack peered over a hedge, thinking exactly what Miles simply came right out and said. He looked at the road leading up the hill to the Stanton Ranch. They were far away enough that they couldn't be seen from the ranch house, but there was a lot of open land with little cover between them and the ranch, from any side, except for the barn, but that would take a while to get around to the back of. Jack shook his head, his hands starting to tremble. He knew what Davis would do if backed into a corner. He'd kill Chris and Helen, if for nothing more than spite, and probably the Stantons as well. Elijah seemed to think the same thing.

"The only way to get those kids out of there is to get *someone* into that house! Once the shooting starts, one person may be able to get them out safely through the chaos!"

Miles nodded his head in agreement from just behind Elijah.

"The Marshal's right, Jack. I hate to put the kids in any more danger, but this Davis fellow will probably keep them close. The chaos may be what saves them."

Blackjack was leaning against a tree just behind them, well covered. He was about to light a cigar, and then caught himself, and slowly put the match back in his pocket, shaking his head.

"That's a dandy idea, boys, but how and who is going to get close enough?"

Miles shifted his weight to his good knee as he peered through the bushes.

"I guess we draw straws, but we better hurry, Jim will be here with the posse any minute, and the night ain't gonna help us any."

Elijah was about to answer that yes, it would, when Godfrey, draped over a horse behind them, whimpered. That whimper was cut short from a gun butt to the head from Blackjack.

"Quiet, you. If we want your opinion about what to do, we'll-wait a minute."

Blackjack and Jack both looked at the prone body of Godfrey and had the same idea.

Why not get two people in?

Tim Hansen chewed the stick of wheat hanging out of his mouth as he watched the road from what must have been the man of houses' bedroom. Hansen had never seen a rich man's home, and hoped to have one like it himself, and he would, once Tarver came up with the money. Hansen stroked the barrel of his rifle gingerly. He started daydreaming of the women that money would give him when he saw two horses approaching. The sun was setting, and could barely make out the figures. He readied his rifle, and yelled back to the other room,

"We got company coming! Two riders!"

Hansen trained his gun on them, and heard Charlie Parks' footsteps as he ran up the steps and into the room. By this time they were near enough to make out. Charlie looked out of the window and the two riders. The first was unmistakable. It was Jack Tarver! Charlie nearly gave Hansen permission to fire when he noticed that the second rider, and the one who had the gun trained on Tarver, was Godfrey! Charlie let out a whoop and ran back to the stairwell.

"Hey Davis! Godfrey's here, and he caught Tarver!"

Blackjack shifted uncomfortably in his saddle as he held the gun on Jack. Godfrey's large hat felt wrong, too. Jack noticed his shifting back and forth.

"Stop that Blackjack, or you'll kill us both!"

"I can't help it! The man has no taste in good clothing! It chafes my delicate skin!"

"For god's sake..."

"Be quiet and keep your hands on the reins, Jack!"

Jack faced forward as they could see Hansen from the window waving them in.

"Come around the back! Man, I'm glad to see you!"

Blackjack almost verbally responded, but instead simply gave Hansen a salute and steered both of them around the back.

Down at the bottom of the hill, Elijah was instructing the ten men who had just arrived about what to do. They readied the two wagons they brought with them, and everyone was soon ready to go. Marshal Elijah Bronson slowly moved the wagons and men quietly up the hill. He knew they had only a minute or less after the two Jacks made it to the ranch to get up the hill and stir some trouble...

Blackjack dismounted his horse first, noting that the other horses were in the nearby stables, and surely there was a man guarding them. He motioned for Jack to get off of his horse, and Jack did so. The back door opened and Charlie peered out from it, waving them in.

"C'mon, hurry in, Godfrey! Man, the boss is hot you took long! But he'll be fine after he sees you got Tarver! How'd you do it?"

Blackjack kept his hat low, covering his face as he pushed Jack toward Charlie, who was six feet away. A bead of sweat ran down Jack's face. Only a few seconds before the kidnapper at the door would recognize it wasn't Godfrey...

Ellie was tense, even more so when she heard Charlie whoop and holler that Jack was coming up the road. She looked to Chris and

Helen, and quickly leaned over to Chris while Davis was ordering Charlie to go out and help Godfrey bring Jack in and whispered to him.

"Keep Helen close, Chris, and you stay with me no matter what!"

Archer overheard this, and wondered what Ellie meant. Ellie sat back up and looked at Consuela, who had just set down more drinks in front of them. Consuela nodded and made her way upstairs, nearly being knocked over as Charlie ran down toward the back kitchen door. She went into Ellie's room, and took the already lit lantern she had left there, and threw it into the closet, and jumped back as the fire shot all over the kerosene-soaked clothes. Consuela closed the door to the room and ran back down the stairs.

Hansen heard the sound of the glass lantern breaking, and from the open door saw Consuela run out of the room, and was about to investigate, when he heard the sounds of wagons. He looked back to the window and ran to it. His veins went icy cold as he saw wagons and riders coming up the hill fast. He ran back to the stairs, nearly following Consuela and yelled.

"Davis! It's the posse! They found us!"

Davis yelled for the men to get ready even as he began to hear Hansen firing his rifle at the approaching posse. Davis saw Consuela run down the stairs and toward the kitchen, and the four men downstairs including Davis began to overturn furniture for cover, while much to Jack and Blackjack's relief Charlie ran back into the house in a panic before noticing who Blackjack wasn't.

Blackjack handed Jack his guns back, and both men quickly pointed their guns at a figure running through the door, but were relieved to see it was Consuela, who they motioned to leave. She ran past them, and into the darkness, and no one ever saw Consuela Martinez again. Upstairs Hansen reloaded his gun and took cover as the window exploded with wood, glass and bullets. The two wagons ran to the front of the house, and the two drivers, one already shot in the arm from Hansen, jumped off of their wagons, and Elijah with the help of a few others dismounted their horses quickly and helped over turn the wagons to avoid the hail of bullets now erupting from the house. Other men including Miles and Jim took positions behind the wagons and started exchanging fire with those inside. The Stanton ranch was alive with sounds of gunfire and missed bullets. Archer and Ellie threw the children to the ground when the shooting started, the living room being destroyed by gunfire. A rain of glass and fabric cascaded down on them, cutting their faces and hands. Hansen had exchanged fire with the last man who passed by his window and started making his way toward the room with the window facing the front when he smelled the smoke, and saw it coming from underneath the door to Ellie's room. Hansen cursed as he opened the door, and singed his eyebrows as the fire from inside jumped out at him. He yelled in surprise and fell down, and Buckner ran from the next room to see what was wrong, and pulled Hansen away by the scruff of his neck as the fire started to spread into the hallway.

Davis was about to yell for Godfrey to get into the fight when several things happened at once. Davis hears Hansen screaming that there's a fire, and then Buckner raced down the stairs, while Charlie ran from the kitchen only to be hit with several bullets from the men outside, and Ellie, Archer and the children ran for the door. Davis' reflexes were faster than his brain as his foot flashed out and tripped Chris as he ran by. Chris fell down, and Helen with him. Ellie reached the door and turned to help them as Archer summoned what little courage he had left and threw himself on Davis. The two men struggled for a moment, and Helen was about to help Chris up when she saw the man who killed her mother, Buckner, running for the kitchen door. Helen looked down at Charlie's dead body and grabbed the gun from his lifeless hand and gave pursuit. Ellie grabbed Chris and helped him up when a shot rang out, and Davis pushed Archer over, and Archer gripped his arm in pain. Davis reached for Chris and grabbed him, pointing the gun at Ellie and smiling. At that moment Jack and

Blackjack were entering the kitchen and ran into Buckner, or rather, Buckner ran over them, bowling both men over as he buffaloed his way through the door and outside. Jack shook his head and grabbed his gun when he and Blackjack saw Helen run by them, following Buckner. Blackjack squinted hard, and saw the gun Helen was holding in her hand. He got up and looked to Jack, who was about to tell him to go after her when two shots rang out from the living room, following Ellie's scream. Blackjack made a decision and ran after Helen. Jack stood up and ran through the kitchen door.

A haze of smoke swept over him from the fire upstairs, and Jack saw Archer on the ground over the body of Ellie, who lied crumpled on the ground. Jack quickly scanned the room. No Chris or Jeremy Davis, but there was a gunman by one of the windows, firing at the posse outside, and then the gunman, Hansen, noticed Jack, and turned to fire, but far too late as Jack snapped a shot at him and hit Hansen in the arm, forcing Hansen to drop the rifle. Jack kept his gun on Hansen as he tried to make out Archer's face as he looked down.

"Archer! Are you all right? What about Ellie?"

Archer looked up, tears in his eyes.

"My angel is dead, Tarver! Davis shot her when she tried to help Chris get away...my dearest angel, my little girl with strawberry hair..."

Archer laid his head down on Ellie's and cried. Jack looked up at Hansen and motioned for him to go outside. Hansen stood up and painfully moved toward the door. Jack yelled for the posse to stop shooting, which they did, and Hansen opened the door and stepped out, with Elijah running forward to tie his hands, and Jack peeked up the stairs, not able to see through the smoke. It was the only place for Davis to go. Jack looked back at the fallen Ellie sadly and slowly made his way up the stairs, and winced as the stairs groaned with his weight. His head snapped up as he heard Davis yell to him.

"Come on up, Jack! Your boy's waitin' for you!"

Jack reached the top of the stairs and carefully looked around the corner. The hallway was ablaze with fire and the smoke was almost blinding Jack, but he could make out the rooms ahead. Jack knew he was in a bad position. Davis surely had the hallway well covered from whichever room he was in. Then again, there was something Davis still needed before he could even think about killing Jack.

"All right, you win, Davis. Just let my boy go and I'll tell you where the gold is!"

He heard a guffaw coming from the second bedroom to the left, across from Ellie's room.

At least now he knew where they were.

"Tell me now, Tarver! Come here and tell me now, or I'll plug your boy!"

Jack walked down the hallway to the room, where the door was halfway opened, and pushed the door open. Through the smoke he saw Davis holding Chris, a gun to Chris' head. Jack raised his gun to Davis, who motioned to it.

"How about you put that gun down, Sergeant Tarver? I'd hate for any thing to happen to you and yours, like that fool Archer downstairs. Did Hansen kill him yet?"

"No."

"Can't find good help when you need it. I must say you surprised me bringing the posse to my doorstep when I could kill your boy at any moment. I could've killed anybody. Like your woman downstairs. She tried to stop me, Jack."

"I can tell you about the gold, but you'll never escape the posse, so it doesn't matter if you know or not."

"Let me worry about them. Start talking, " said Davis, cocking the hammer on the gun. Jack looked to Chris, who looked fearful, but at the same time had that Tarver defiance.

"I'm here now, son. You'll be fine. Davis, here's some of that gold for you."

Jack fished into his pocket and tossed the object at Davis, who caught it and looked at it. A gold necklace with the picture of a pretty, if not outright beautiful woman.

"The hell's this?"

"The treasure you wanted so badly. That map we found at Virginia Hills? It was treasure of a sort. That cave in Colorado was full of that family's most prized possessions: their family painting and heirlooms handed down through the years. Furniture, clothing, and this was the only gold to be found there. Now you have it all."

Davis stared at the pendant. The only gold there was? He lost his family and life over this? Davis' hand trembled with rage as he clutched the pendent tightly in his hand and looked up. Jack knew he would have to get lucky now, and could feel the fire spreading nearer. It had engulfed the hallway he had just come down, and no doubt was already spreading into the room. Jack wiped the sweat from his brow as he readied himself for something Sam would have probably called an incredibly stupid move. Davis yelled in rage and pointed the gun at Jack. Chris pushed the gun hand up as it fired, and Jack launched himself at Davis, knocking the gun out of his hand. Chris dropped to the floor as Jack punched Davis, who staggered back and returned with a punch to the stomach, and ran Jack's head into the wooden dresser drawer behind them. Chris stood up and ran toward the door, and saw the fire entering the room, and jumped back. He frantically looked toward the window, and pushed the window doors open, and Miles had to stop from firing at the window as he saw Chris and yelled to the men. Elijah looked up as several men grabbed the bound Hansen, and pointed at Chris.

"It's Chris! Get one of the wagons! Fill it with hay and get it under there! Hurry!"

Three men turned one of the wagons back on its wheels and started grabbing bales of hay that were thankfully nearby, and loaded it into the wagon. Meanwhile, Elijah then heard a shot ring out, but not from within the house, but behind it. He grabbed a nearby rifle and ran for the back of the house.

Davis threw himself on Jack once again in a rage, and Jack threw a punch at Davis, hitting him square in the jaw, and Davis fell back to the ground, and Jack knew he had made a mistake the moment he did it, as Davis fell next to his gun. Jack noticed that Davis' gun was on the floor just in front of him. Jack reached for the gun as Davis grabbed his, and Davis yelled in pain as Chris kicked him in the face. Davis fell over in a heap, and didn't move. Jack ran over and quickly hugged Chris and looked around as the fire had now begun to spread into the room. Chris motioned for Jack to go to the window, and he looked out and saw the wagon filled with hay below. Some men standing around it waved at Chris to jump. Jack motioned for Chris to go first, and Chris stepped out of the window and jumped from the sill, and landed unhurt on the hay. Several men pulled Chris out of the wagon and yelled for Jack to jump down. Jack walked over and grabbed Davis first and carried him to the window. He dropped Davis out of the window next, and waited for the men to pull him off of the wagon, and then jumped out himself. He landed in the hay and seemed to almost bounce out as he and Chris ran back to where the posse were, and were greeted by Miles and Jim Daly, who slapped Jack on the back. Doc Harrison started looking Chris over, and Chris looked beside one of the wagons and saw Archer kneeling on the ground in front of what must be the body of poor Ellie. Chris looked at his father, who was staring at the departed Ellie. There was sadness behind those brown eyes despite his cool demeanor. One more moment of pain for his father. Chris' thoughts then turned to another red-haired girl. He looked back at Miles and Jim.

"Where's Helen?"

Buckner ran as fast as he could when he saw the fire break out. There was no way Davis was gonna get his money now. He ran down the stairs and thought that Hansen had followed him, and he didn't even notice the two men he knocked down in the kitchen as he ran out of the door toward the stables. Hopefully he could get away in the confusion, and be out of the state by sunrise. Any thoughts of escaped left Buckner as he heard a gunshot not far behind him. He stopped running and turned to face his attacker. He almost laughed as he looked at the little girl in front of him, but a chill ran down his spine as he saw the murderous look in her eyes, and the gun pointed at him. He reached for his own gun and felt the empty holster. He must have dropped it when he was running out of the house! Buckner put his hands up.

"Okay, little lady, you got me. How about you just hand me that gun before you hurt yourself with it?"

Helen didn't answer at first, just kept the gun pointed at Buckner. She could barely hear Buckner, only hearing her mother's scream as she was shot. She looked down at the gun and cocked the hammer back as she saw some of the other kidnappers do. She looked back at Buckner, who was now frozen in fear.

"C'mon, girl, your ma was an accident! She tried to fight me, see? The gun went off..."

Helen took a step forward, the tears coursing down her red cheeks like a waterfall. This man took away the last thing she had in the world, and at least she could avenge her mother.

"I don't care. You killed her. She didn't do anything! *We* didn't do anything! You came and took her away from me, and now you'll pay!"

Helen aimed the gun and was about to shoot when she heard a voice behind her.

"Are you sure you want to do this, Ms. Miller?"

Helen looked behind her and saw Blackjack, and quickly turned back to Buckner, who was now thoroughly convinced he was about to die.

Blackjack put his gun away, and stepped forward confidently.

"Of course I do. He killed my Ma!" she said.

"Yeah, and Buckner here deserves death, after getting tried in court, darlin'. You can't just kill a man like this."

"You did. I heard about it."

Blackjack shook his head and tilted his Godfrey's hat back.

"That's different. The man tried to pull a gun on me first. It was fair and square. What you're about to do won't make you any better than them. Killing an unarmed man? What would your Pa say if he were here?"

Helen's hands trembled as she looked back at Blackjack.

"You don't know my father!"

"True, but I know what kind of man he was. Gave up his life tryin' to get the money for your medicine. What he did was wrong, but his reasons anyone could understand. But, he didn't try to save you so you could become a killer. They raised you to be better than that. You pull that trigger and you'll truly have lost everything."

Helen started crying, and Blackjack walked toward her as she slowly lowered the gun. Blackjack gingerly took the gun from her hand as Marshal Bronson walked past them and started tying Buckner's hands behind his back. Helen grabbed Blackjack and hugged him, the tears of anger and sadness flowing from her freely now, Blackjack was taken aback at this. He wasn't used to dealing with...emotions. He awkwardly put his arms around Helen and hugging her back.

"Now *that* will make your parents proud of you."

Elijah, pushing a grumbling Buckner past them, looked at Blackjack, and couldn't help but grin.

"Now I've done seen everything. You're actually human, aren't you, Blackjack?"

"Don't tell anyone, Marshal. You'll ruin my reputation."

Together they made their way back toward the burning house, and the relieved people waiting for them.

Chapter 16: The Saints of Liberty

Marshal Elijah Bronson stepped out of his office to do his afternoon walk through town. The streets were a bustle as normal, and people were smiling, and Elijah felt himself smiling as well. It had been a full month since the incident at Stanton Ranch, and the town looked as if it was recovering nicely. It had been somber for quite a few weeks after the burials of both Patricia Miller and Eleanor Stanton. There was healing to be done, and it was well along, and the town would be stronger for it, he was sure. One of the first things they did was to tear down the house at Harvey's Hill once and for all, and decided to rename it Spivey's Hill, in memory of Sam. Doc Harrison waved at Elijah as he rode his horse down the street, on his way to deliver a baby at the Parker homestead. Elijah then passed by the Yellow Saloon, where he saw Blackjack tipping his hat to him, just having played two miners out of their gold. Elijah frowned back. It was only a matter of time before whatever Blackjack was running from caught up with him. Why else would he be in such a small, but growing town? He did help save Chris and Helen, so that at least bought him the benefit of the doubt with Elijah. Barely.

Elijah's walk took him by the bank, where Jim Daley and his wife were taking off for the day. Jim was all smiles, and waved at the Marshal. Elijah waved back and wished them a good day, and continued on until he reached Miles' smithy. Miles was putting the finishing touches on a new rifle upgraded for Farmer Tom Jordan, when he looked up and greeted Elijah.

"How do, Marshal? It's a fine day, a fine day indeed!"

"You're right about that, Miles. Say, did you finish that gun for Jack?"

Miles nodded his head and reached on his shelf and brought down the new gun, now with the engraving that says the 'Saints of Liberty' on it. The marshal took the gun and looked at it for a moment. Since Jack had lost Sam's gun in the fire, getting him a new one was the least they could do for him, between saving the bank and stopping the Davis Gang.

"That's a beautiful job, Miles. Probably your best work ever! I'm headed out to Jack's place. I'll make sure he gets it."

Two hours later found Elijah riding up the road taking him to Jack's place, passing the Miller homestead. Archer Stanton emerged from around the back of the barn, and nodded at the marshal as he passed by. Elijah smiled at this. Since Ellie died, Archer sold his entire ranch to pay off his debtors, and had just enough money to buy the Miller homestead, and immediately took Helen into his home. They seem to like each other well enough, and Elijah was happy about that. Stanton lost his daughter and gained another, and Helen gained a new...uncle, as he liked to be called. The strength of Helen inspired the entire town. She lost everything, and yet she still smiles when she and Stanton are in town.

Elijah came up to the Tarver ranch and pulled his horse into the dirt walk to the house. Chris and Helen were cleaning up the house, and both came out to greet Elijah.

"Hey Marshal!" they both almost shouted in unison.

"Good to see you two kids all in smiles. Where's your Pa, Chris?"

"He's feeding the horses. What can we do for you?"

"Oh, I just came to visit for a bit." Elijah lied.

He didn't want to say more, and didn't have to as Manny and Alex Peacock ran through the field, calling out to them.

"Hey, ya'll there's the biggest frog you ever did see down at the creek! C'mon before it gets away!" yelled Manny.

Chris and Helen were both relieved the Peacock Brothers showed up. Ever since that night with the Davis gang, they felt guilty, but right not to tell the Marshal, or anyone else, about what really happened that night, and the part Archer Stanton ultimately played. He wound up losing the very thing he fought so hard to protect, and that was punishment enough. Besides, Helen and Archer were getting along fine, so why ruin that? Archer saw a lot of Ellie in Helen, and Helen saw the kind, but tough man her father used to be before things got bad for them. Chris and Helen ran after the Peacock Brothers, laughing all the way, and Elijah made his way to the stables, where he saw Jack feeding the last of his horses.

"Ho there, Jack! Brought something for you. Consider it a thank you from the folks of Liberty."

Jack looked up just as Elijah tossed the gun to him. Jack deftly caught the gun with one hand. Elijah leaned against the entrance as he regarded this.

"Good reflexes, Jack. Not many can move like that, not anymore, anyway. Not many experienced like that."

Jack marveled at the sheer beauty of the gun and then set the gun down on a nearby barrel and started putting hay in the horse stall.

"You trying to say something, Marshal?"

"Yes I am. You aren't just a father making a new start, nor are you just a war veteran, either. You're also a gunfighter. Probably one of the last out there."

"*Was* a gunfighter. That life is over now. After I married Elizabeth, that life ended."

Elijah nodded his head.

"Nevertheless, some young fools may yet try to make a name off of killing you. I did some checking around on you back in Texas. Killed a lot of men, all fair fights and for good reasons, just like with Davis and his gang."

"I didn't kill Davis."

"No, and I hear Judge Harper ordered the gallows for him, as if that were any surprise. Godfrey's already swung, and the others will be doing some prison time."

Jack put his pitchfork down and grabbed the gun, and walked back toward the house with Elijah.

"So I take it you want to make sure I don't cause any more trouble here. I promise you, Marshal, I won't. I wanted a good place to raise my son in peace, and the people of Liberty are some of the best people I've ever met."

"I know, Jack, and we're glad to have you, and you're welcome to stay, but I worry if any more of your past comes stomping in here. You and Blackjack both worry me a bit in that regard."

Jack didn't answer, because he didn't have one.

"I just want to know, if it does come to that, will you stand as you did against Davis and his gang?"

"Yes."

"Good, but you'll probably need this."

Jack turned and looked down as Elijah's hand held out a deputy's badge.

"I can't take that, Elijah."

"You don't have a choice, Jack. I'm getting old, Jack, and if trouble-yours or anyone else's- does come I may need some help, and you're the best help there is. You think I should give this to Blackjack instead?"

Jack shook his head and took the badge from Elijah and looked at it, and then looked back up and smiled.

"It's a deal, Elijah, but only if trouble is here, if not, I'll be here tending the ranch."

"Deal, son. Now that *that's* over, I hear tells you make a pretty good cup of coffee, and I also bet you have a few funny stories about our Sam!"

Jack smiled and guided Elijah into the house. He gripped the badge, and hoped he wouldn't have to use it, but he would to protect the town of Liberty-the only family Sam's ever had. Elijah just hoped he had made the right decision.

He didn't have to wait long to find out.

Not the End.

Don't miss out!

Visit the website below and you can sign up to receive emails whenever Michael Moore publishes a new book. There's no charge and no obligation.

https://books2read.com/r/B-A-GFPS-CXMWB

BOOKS 2 READ

Connecting independent readers to independent writers.

About the Author

Michael Moore is writer and filmmaker from Texas who has a love for three things: martial arts, westerns, and a great cheeseburger. Michael wrote the comic books *El Gato Negro: Legacy* and *Team Tejas,* and also wrote, directed and edited the short action films *El Gato Negro: Prey* and *Cornered.* Michael is currently writing his second novel Message in the Dark before starting on the next adventure of Jack Tarver and the Liberty Saints. He currently lives in Texas with his wife and two sons.